WILL DUREY

# ARKANSAS BUSHWHACKERS

*Complete and Unabridged*

## LINFORD
*Leicester*

First published in Great Britain in 2015 by
Robert Hale Limited
London

First Linford Edition
published 2016
by arrangement with
Robert Hale Limited
London

A catalogue record for this book is available
from the British Library.

ISBN 978–1–4448–2932–7

Published by
F. A. Thorpe (Publishing)
Anstey, Leicestershire

Set by Words & Graphics Ltd.
Anstey, Leicestershire
Printed and bound in Great Britain by
T. J. International Ltd., Padstow, Cornwall

This book is printed on acid-free paper

# ARKANSAS BUSHWHACKERS

Former Union soldier Charlie Jefferson strikes up a friendship with Dave and Henry Willis in Pottersville, Arkansas. The brothers are planning to drive cattle from Texas to the lumber camps of the Arkansas timberland, and invite Charlie to join them. But the scheme falls foul of the Red Masks, a gang of bushwhackers who are terrorizing the area. To bring the criminals to justice, Charlie must throw in his lot with the army once more . . .

# 1

Some units of the VI Corps had joined General Sheridan's command that morning and were held in reserve while the enemy, half-a-mile away, tried to repel the cavalry charges. The fight had begun with Sheridan's field guns bombarding the Confederate line. There had been little response to the salvo — an indication that most of the rebels' artillery had been abandoned at Petersburg — but occasionally a Confederate cannon shell would scream its way towards the ranks of blue, a defiant retaliation for the destruction that was being meted out to their own army.

Then Sheridan unleashed his cavalry in a series of charges that almost overwhelmed the foe. The South responded with their handful of howitzers, such punishing weapons when discharged at close quarters, barking out spherical case shot and canister which spread from the mouth of the weapon like buckshot from oversized shotguns, devastating to both onrushing horses and riders. When the cavalry pulled back to re-organize, the big guns of the North roared again.

The South's resistance couldn't last long. Another concentrated cavalry attack broke through the enemy line and that was the signal for the infantry, including the units of the VI Corps, to join the fray. With the smoke of their own shells drifting back towards them they swarmed across the dividing ground to grapple hand-to-hand with the enemy.

Below the smoke, here and there along the battlefront, white flags of surrender could be seen among the grey ranks of Confederate soldiers. Now and then, rifle shots crackled, marking the small resistance points that were eventually overrun and scattered by the merciless cavalry charges, but the big guns were quiet and to all intents and purposes the Battle of Sayler's Creek was over.

* * *

For three days, since the failure of their defence of Petersburg and in compliance with General Lee's subsequent orders, the rebels had marched west determined to link up with General Johnson's army in North Carolina, but every step of the way had been dogged by battles and skirmishes with the better supplied and equipped Union army. Now, with the loss of this battle, a quarter of their remaining force had been captured and the end of the war was imminent.

But there were Union casualties, too, that day, grotesque bundles in blue cloth were scattered across a landscape pitted with canister detonations and scarred by mounted charges. For these dead, dying and wounded soldiers, the end of hostilities had not come soon enough. Among them lay Charlie

Jefferson, a soldier in the VI Corps, his upper body ripped open by shrapnel but his life preserved by a vigilant medic and a swift transfer to Hillsman House which had been pressed into service as a field hospital.

Three days passed before Charlie regained consciousness and even that was for barely a few minutes. The noise in the hospital, the cries of men in agony, made him think he was still in the midst of battle where yells and shrieks mingled with bugle calls, drum rolls, gunshots and explosions. Although there was no clarity to his thoughts, no specific memory that governed this brief moment of consciousness, his immediate concern was for his friend Amos Prescott. Finding Amos was an overwhelming need. At one moment as they ran through the thick smoke towards the ever-nearing rifle flashes of the enemy, they had been side-by-side, then he was gone.

'Amos,' he called and at the same time tried to turn to his left where he expected his friend to be.

'Careful,' someone said, and that person put a tin cup to his lips and allowed a few drops of cold water to moisten them.

'Where's Amos?'

'Don't know,' said the other. 'Got enough to do fixing you up, pal. You've been hit bad but if you take it easy you'll pull through.'

Charlie heard the words but his brain couldn't juggle them into sense, and why was someone giving him a drink in the middle of a battle? The smell of gunpowder and blood momentarily flooded his senses but was quickly replaced by an odd sensation, as though a great weight was pressing on his chest. He wanted to ask again about Amos but he was engulfed by blackness and it was another day before he gained a grasp on reality again. This time when he turned his head to the left he saw a familiar face.

'How you doing?' asked Fess Salter. Fess was a grizzled fellow, formerly a trapper and trader who had acted as guide and interpreter for military expeditions in the highlands of the west before enlisting in the Union cause. He'd begun to bivouac with Charlie and Amos when he learned they were from the Wyoming Territory. They'd all agreed that westerners should stick together.

Fess spoke again. 'You took a bad hit, Charlie, and lost a lot of blood. Thought you might not make it for a while but the doctor says you'll do.' He began to grin to add conviction to the fact that his words carried good news but it didn't spread across his face because he remembered that Charlie always told him that he was the only person he'd met who looked less pleasant when grinning.

Charlie let his tongue run over his dry lips and Fess took the hint and found a cup to give him a drink. 'War's over,' he told Charlie. 'Lee surrendered two days ago. Custer captured his supply train at Appomattox Station, leaving him with no choice in the matter.'

Charlie shuffled, winced then closed his eyes for a moment to hide the pain from his friend.

'When you get out that bed we're going home,' Fess said.

'Where's Amos?' Charlie's voice was almost unrecognizable, thin now, reedy but demanding an answer.

'He's gone, Charlie.'

'He was at my side,' Charlie explained, recalling once again his last battlefield memory before being lifted into the air by a nearby explosion. 'One moment we were together and the next he wasn't there. That's why I stopped. I looked around but couldn't find him.'

Fess stood and rested his hand on his young friend's arm. 'You build up your strength then we'll get out of this place. Head back west where we belong.'

But Charlie wasn't listening; his thoughts were fixed on the valley of his home. 'What will I tell his folks?' he muttered. 'What will I tell them?'

★ ★ ★

In 1854, when Charlie was ten years old, his family had settled in the valley of the Tatanka, a tributary which fed the North Platte. They were accompanied by eight other families including that of Amos Prescott. Early successive hard winters became a trial of endurance which eventually persuaded two of those other families to move further west to the warmer climes of California.

For those who remained their lives were industrious but, in the main, content. Cattle herds increased and, after the disaster of the first two winters, their vegetable crops yielded sufficient to satisfy each family. The sale of steers and excess vegetables was negotiated with the military at Fort Laramie and cattle were driven there twice a year.

Without professional people in their group the settlers developed their own creed for existence. All matters were

8

resolved within the valley. They tended their own ailments, settled their own disputes, buried their own dead and taught their offspring the things they needed to know to help the family prosper. Those that came later to the valley, if they stayed, were obliged to abide by the decisions of the first settlers but they were only welcome if they were prepared to work for one of the existing ranchers. No one else was permitted to run cattle on the range. Some came and stayed, finding employment on one of the spreads. Others came, worked a summer roundup then drifted on again. Only one man, a man called Grice, tried to buck the rule, tried running cattle on Jefferson range, but he failed. His beasts were confiscated and when he returned with a bunch of armed men he encountered a united force of valley families. All the invaders were buried where they fell, making the message clear: This valley was spoken for. There was no room for anyone else.

Charlie was fifteen at that time and the settlers were finally beginning to show some prosperity. The herds were larger, outbuildings more numerous and hired hands on the increase. Drifters, having heard of the valley from tales passed on by wagon scouts and soldiers, rode in, but only those with the intention of finding work on one or other of the ranches ever stayed. A trading post had been established at a river crossing point and Sam Flint, its proprietor, would sell a jug of whisky to anyone who could pay for it, but his establishment wasn't a saloon bar where men could gather to play cards or dally with dance-hall girls. Without those attractions there was nothing to persuade drifters to stay.

Two years later, war was declared and although in the main the people of the Tatanka Valley considered the conflict primarily the concern of those in the east, Charlie saw it as a chance for adventure, sure that the fighting would soon be over. His father didn't want him to enlist but soon realized that his son's determination could not be overcome. When he left the valley in the spring of 1862 his friend Amos went with him.

Ezra Prescott, Amos's father, never ceased to oppose his son's decision, insisting that there were enough battles to fight if they were to establish the homestead. Most of those battles were against nature and the climate but rustlers and Indian raids were not unknown. Unlike Charlie, Amos believed in the cause he chose to fight for but his father refused to acknowledge his son's political argument, that the spread of slavery to the west would prevent their own enterprise flourishing. Their parting was acrimonious and Ezra heaped plenty of the blame for that on Charlie Jefferson.

Both Charlie and Amos had brothers and Amos had a sister, too, and it was blonde-haired Ruth who mainly filled Charlie's thoughts as he lay on his hospital bed. Ruth had been his girl before he quit the valley and had promised to be waiting for him when he returned with the fortune he believed he'd accrue while pursuing the great adventure. The memory of Ruth had helped him through many desolate moments during the campaigns of the past three years and warmed his nights when shivering under canvas in muddy and icy fields. He had no doubt of her constancy but he couldn't escape the fact that returning penniless and without her brother would throw a pall over his homecoming.

When he was able he sent off three letters to the valley of the Tatanka River. The first, to Ezra Prescott, was the most difficult to write. Attempting to explain Amos's death didn't come easy and he hoped he would better convey his own sense of loss when he and Ezra met face to face. The only message that his letters to Ruth and his parents bore was that he was heading home. He didn't say that the journey would be extended until he had enough money to fulfil his promise to Ruth, nor did he include any information which would let them know how to contact him. For the moment, until he'd shaken off the memories of war's violence and until he'd come to terms with his own survival, he needed to be alone.

So when he left hospital he explained to Fess why he wouldn't immediately be heading west.

Fess rubbed his jaw. 'Have you got some plan for making this fortune you mean to take home with you?'

Charlie shook his head. 'I heard tell that there was plenty of work in Petersburg. Clearing away rubble; rebuilding homes.'

'You won't get rich by hiring yourself out on a daily basis,' Fess argued. 'It'll take the rest of your life to build a bankroll in that fashion.'

'It's a starting point,' Charlie told him. 'I'll find something better. There will be opportunities.'

Fess didn't agree. 'There'll be little money in a war-ravaged town and what there is will be gobbled up by crooks and politicians. Move on, Charlie. Go home. The war went on longer than anyone expected. Your girl and family will be pleased enough to see you.'

Charlie's mind was set, however, although he wasn't sure if his reluctance to return home was due to his lack of fortune or the loss of Amos. What he did know was that if others expected to be hailed as returning heroes it was an epithet he felt unable to wear. Even Fess's unsubtle hint that his injures could have left him incapable of such heavy manual work could not sway him from his intention. He would find employment in Petersburg.

Two days before they were mustered out the army Fess again brought up the subject of making money. 'Got to talking with Colonel Crook yesterday,' he began. Fess had known Colonel Crook out at Fort Laramie, had acted as his scout when patrolling the Oregon Trail to ensure the safe westward passage of immigrants. 'He's looking for men to help round up the remaining rebels. Are you interested?'

Charlie shook his head. 'I've had enough of the army.'

'You wouldn't be in the army. He wants civilians to mix with local communities and find these fellows. Dangerous work so the pay will be better than you'd get clearing rubble. What do you say?'

'Is that what you intend doing?'

Fess rubbed in characteristic fashion at his whiskery jaw. 'You know I'm hankering to get back to the high country,' he said, 'but I'll do it if you will.'

Charlie thought for a moment. 'I think I've had enough fighting. I'm not looking for that sort of trouble, Fess. Those fellows will surrender soon enough when they see everyone else at peace.'

'Reckon so,' said Fess. 'Reckon so.'

* * *

A week later Fess had ridden away towards the Territories beyond the Mississippi and Charlie had made the short journey east to the ruined city of Petersburg where he stayed for less than three weeks. It didn't take him long to realize that he wasn't welcome in Virginia. Finding work wasn't difficult; he was an ex-Union soldier and the men who held sway in the conquered state were northern speculators prepared to grasp every opportunity to humiliate the people of the south. If that meant pushing them towards starvation by depriving them of jobs then that was one of the benefits of the war; to the victor the spoils.

It was a state of affairs that Charlie couldn't long tolerate although he knew that quitting his job was no guarantee that he would be replaced by an ex-soldier of the south. But quit he did, mainly because, as Fess had predicted, what he was being paid was barely enough to sustain him through the week and therefore no road to the riches he hoped to take back to Ruth Prescott.

However, one thing that did improve was his physical strength. His body showed many scars, front and back. Some would disappear in time but others were long and ugly and during the first few days of loading debris on to carts in Petersburg they subjected him to such agony that he feared himself incapable of such labour but, by the time he, too, rode west from Virginia, further worries about the damage that had been done to his body were cast from his mind. He knew he was stronger than he had ever been.

# 2

From May to August Charlie Jefferson rode west with no destination in mind and no plan for acquiring the wealth he sought. Across Virginia and Kentucky he wandered, touching small towns where he hoped to earn enough to keep him fed and provisioned for the next phase of his journey. Wherever he travelled the effects of the war were clear to see and at most of his stopping places he was viewed with suspicion whenever his conversation made it clear he had fought for the Union. Men from the north were suspected of being carpetbaggers, opportunists looking to buy up southern estates for a fraction of their true worth. Consequently, when he arrived in a town where it was evident that there was insufficient work for homecoming Confederate soldiers, he quickly moved on. He heard rumours of work in the Arkansas timberland and, although that meant heading further south than he intended, his money was low and he was attracted by the prospect of earning a regular income for a while.

Three days after crossing the Arkansas River, dry, hungry and dust-covered, Charlie reined in his mount on a bluff above an arid canyon that opened out to the plains land beyond. Ahead, as far as the eye could see, the scrubby land stretched, unchanging, until, he supposed, it became Texas. The high rock face of the opposite canyon wall obscured any view to the south but he hoped that somewhere close at hand there was a town or settlement which would provide a comfortable bed for at least one night. His most pressing need, however, was a clear stream which would refresh both him and his horse.

As he removed his hat and wiped his brow with his sleeve something below caught his eye. Smoke was rising like a thin, pale ribbon, carrying with it the smell of pine logs. To his surprise and pleasure he discovered that the smoke emanated from the stone-built chimney of a mainly log-built house, an indication that a small corner of civilization was close at hand. The building was almost directly below, clinging to the shadow at the mouth of the canyon, making its presence difficult to detect from Charlie's position. He stepped his horse forward until he was on the brink of the precipice where he was more able to study the set-up below.

Although the dryness of the territory seemed to preclude the growing of crops, the layout was that of a farm. A number of other buildings of variable size were clustered around the house, the function of each easily identifiable. There was a stable, barn, bunkhouse and out-buildings but, unlike the house, each bore the air of abandonment that he had seen so often during recent weeks. At one time this might have been a thriving farm but now it was in disrepair, another home in decline because of the war.

A series of low-fenced pens stretching into the open scrubland stood empty and many of the timber poles with which they were constructed were broken or dislodged. In contrast, however, a high fenced corral between the house and stable was in good repair. Thirty or more horses mingled quietly within but Charlie could discern no other activity around the place. Neither cattle nor sheep could be seen grazing in the scrubland, there was no dog on the prowl or hens scratching at the dirt. However, Charlie saw something in the yard that caused him to prick his horse into finding a way to the valley below. In front of the house stood a well and the prospect of cold water caused Charlie to run his tongue over his dry lips.

A fence had been built to enclose the buildings and, like the horse corral, it remained intact. In order to reach the long gate which gave access to the yard Charlie had to ride around and approach the farm from the scrubland. At the gate he called out to the house but no one answered. When his second call got no response his thirst took the upper hand over customary practice. He could wait no longer for an invitation into the yard. Reaching forward he grasped the loop that was holding the gate closed. Without warning a shot rang out from the side of the building. A huge chunk of wood flew out of the gatepost and spun through the air eventually digging deep into the hind quarters of Charlie's horse.

The horse squealed and twisted, at first sinking back on its hind legs then jerking upright as though preparing to kick out at its torment. Charlie was caught off-guard both by the gunshot and the horse's reaction but by shortening the reins he endeavoured to bring the beast under control.

'Whoa, boy,' he called. Involuntarily, his voice came out louder and rougher than normal which invoked the adverse effect to what Charlie had intended and the horse tried to fling its head to the side to break free of Charlie's hold. With more gentleness in his voice, Charlie spoke again and at the same time ran the flat of his hand down the animal's neck to reassure it. Snorting, the horse gave a little jump, all hoofs clearing the ground like a rodeo bronco. The landing jarred its body and excited another painful spasm. Its eyes rolled, frightened by the injury and the restraining hold of its rider.

Charlie spoke once more, could feel the horse quiver beneath him and knew that its desire to bolt was subsiding. He wanted to dismount and check the wound but he was aware of movement at the other side of the fence and knew that if flight was necessary his best hope of survival was to stay on board. With his horse almost under control Charlie was able to spare a glance in the direction of his adversary and was concerned by what he saw.

Once the shot had been fired, the shooter had flung aside the old Hall single-shot rifle and grabbed a similar gun which had been propped against the side of the house. Now the woman stalked across the yard with the second loaded gun pointed squarely at Charlie's body. She was a long woman and although the jacket she wore over a soiled, grey dress added some bulk to her body it was clear that the flesh on her bones was sparse. On her head she wore an old, broad-brimmed hat and short laced-up black boots on her feet but it was the fierceness of her expression that demanded most attention. Her face was long and lined with the cares of almost sixty years of life and her unblinking eyes were like chips of hard rock. Her mouth was long and narrow-lipped and it turned down at the extremes, marking a determination to finish what she'd started. Her finger tightened on the trigger of the long rifle.

The thought of bringing out his

pistol from its military, flap-covered holster lingered with Charlie no longer than a second. Not only did the prospect of drawing a gun on a woman sit uneasily with him but he knew that she could pull the trigger a lot more quickly than he could arm himself. He knew that if she pulled the trigger he was a dead man because he was convinced that there had been no element of luck in her first shot; she had struck the gate post exactly where she'd aimed to hit it.

'Hold there,' he shouted, raising his left hand while keeping a firm grip on the reins in his right hand. 'I'm not seeking trouble.'

'Then ride on,' the woman commanded. 'Keep off my land.'

'I called out but you didn't answer.'

'Doesn't mean you can trespass on my property.' She gestured with the rifle for him to ride away.

'I just wanted a drink from your well. Some water for me and the horse. We've been travelling awhile. Hoped you'd be able to tell us how far it is to the next town.'

'Yankee, ain't you?' The enmity in the woman's voice was unmistakeable. Her eyes shifted fleetingly but meaningfully towards the buttoned-down holster Charlie wore military-style on his left hip.

There was no denying its association with the Union army so Charlie didn't try to. 'I fought for the Union but the war is over.'

'I heard,' the woman said, 'the lies they're spreading that General Lee surrendered.'

'It's not a lie, ma'am,' Charlie told her. 'He surrendered back in Virginia.'

Her head lifted an inch. There was pride in the movement but obstinacy, too. 'The south will never surrender,' she told Charlie. 'When the last of our ammunition has been fired we'll fight on with sticks and stones, like the boys did at Sayler's Creek.'

Charlie had known of incidents when rebels without firearms had attacked with cudgels and stones but they had mostly been deserters hoping to get home without being caught by soldiers of either side, and he knew for a fact that that had not been the case at Sayler's Creek.

'Nobody fought with sticks and stones that day, ma'am.'

The woman's eyes narrowed. 'Were you there?'

'I was.'

'One of my sons was killed there,' she said, 'murdered by Sherman's butchers when he had nothing left to fight with.'

Her arms moved, slowly, making it obvious to Charlie that she was contemplating pulling the trigger; that his life could be over with a twitch of her finger. Even so, he refused to agree with her. He hadn't fought for three years in order to deny the Union's exploits when victory had been achieved.

'My best friend died there, too,' he told her, 'and he wasn't clubbed to death by unarmed men. The Confederates had powder and shot enough that day, they were just weary and outnumbered.'

For several moments the pair faced each other in silence, she holding her long rifle with unwavering determination and he, now that his animal had ceased its fidgeting, as still as a monument, resolved not to back down from her threatened violence.

'If you kill me it will be murder,' he told her, 'and one day you will have to pay for it.' The woman didn't speak, nor did she put up the weapon but Charlie sensed that her moment for pulling the trigger had passed. 'You wounded my horse,' he said raising his eyes to look at the corral full of animals behind her. 'I'd appreciate exchanging him for one of those.'

'I need my stock,' she said. 'Ride on.'

'What about a drink from the well?'

'Ride on,' she repeated. 'Yankees aren't welcome here.'

'The horse isn't a Yankee,' he told her. 'Bought him in Virginia. He needs a drink.'

Her answer was a jerk of the rifle, a forceful gesture to send him on his way. 'There's a stream three miles on,' she told Charlie. 'He should make it that far.'

Realizing that further conversation would achieve nothing, Charlie turned the horse and headed at walking gait into the scrubland. As he rode away the hairs on his neck prickled, at any second he expected a bullet in his back. When he'd covered four hundred yards he looked back over his shoulder. The woman had only moved to rest the barrel of her rifle on the top rail around the yard and the way she watched his progress made it clear that she wouldn't hesitate to shoot him if he chose to return.

Charlie didn't stop until he'd covered more than a mile, far enough to be out of range of the old Hall rifle. He'd wanted to stop sooner, had wanted to examine the damage to his horse and remove the splinter which was still sticking in its flesh. Now and then it had turned its head to look back along its body trying to see the offending object that was causing irritation with each stride. However, when Charlie dismounted and removed the wedge of wood he found the damage slight. After a few words of comfort he remounted and at a steady canter they journeyed on until they reached the stream whose existence Charlie had half doubted.

Refreshed, they moved on, southward in the direction of the timberland until Charlie's attention was drawn to dust rising in the east, an indication that he was not the only traveller in the territory. He headed in that direction and along a rutted trail he met six men with a couple of heavily loaded wagons. They had seen him while they were yet some distance apart and those who weren't handling the teams demonstrated wariness for the lone rider by watching his approach with unflinching gaze and primed rifles on show.

Charlie waited at the side of the trail until the front wagon reached him then he turned to ride alongside. The driver didn't slow the team, didn't cast a look in Charlie's direction, left the conversation to the man seated beside him on the high-board. The guard at the rear of the wagon was now standing, his rifle menacingly trained on Charlie but his attention seemed to be on the scrubland beyond, as though he expected other riders to pop up out of nowhere.

'What's your destination?' Charlie asked.

The front guard motioned forward with his head. 'Pottersville,' he said. 'Are you travelling alone?'

Charlie said he was. 'You'd have seen the dust if I was with others.'

The man uttered a sound that was no more than a grunt, a grudging acceptance of the truth in Charlie's words. 'Have you got business in Pottersville?' he asked.

'No, just hoping to find a comfortable bed. I've spent a lot of nights sleeping on the ground.'

'Were you a soldier?'

If the recent confrontation with the woman at the farm was a guide to the general feelings in this area then Charlie knew that admitting his involvement could ignite a powder keg of trouble but, as earlier, he wasn't prepared to deny his actions no matter who disapproved of them. 'I fought for the Union,' he told his questioner. The information didn't seem to disturb the man or his companions, indeed Charlie sensed the tension ease as he rode with them. 'My name's Charlie Jefferson from the Wyoming Territory.'

'You're a long way from home, Charlie,' said the man. 'Are you looking for work?'

'I heard there was plenty in the timberlands. That's where I'm heading.'

The man laughed. 'You're going in the wrong direction,' he said, indicating over his shoulder. 'South is that way.'

'I know,' Charlie told him, 'but if Pottersville is the nearest town then that's the place for me. My horse needs a rest and I need some lively company.' The guard and driver exchanged meaningful glances which were seen by Charlie. 'What is it?' he asked.

'Just hope the town doesn't get too hot for you.'

'Why should it?'

'Red Masks,' said the driver and when Charlie seemed unfamiliar with the term he added, 'Rebels, Confederates who haven't surrendered and are waging their own war against carpetbaggers.'

'What is their connection with Pottersville?'

'No connection, yet,' the guard told Charlie, 'but a lot of people there are working up a panic that Pottersville will be the next place that is attacked. A lot of land has been bought up and businesses taken over by men from the north.'

'What is the army doing about it?' asked Charlie.

'Not much,' said the driver. 'There

are a lot of these bands roaming throughout Arkansas, Kansas and Missouri. By the time the army arrive at a scene of an attack another incident occurs somewhere else.'

Charlie was bemused by this unofficial continuation of the war. When hostilities ended he had had his own reasons for not returning home immediately but he was pleased that the fighting was over. But he had fought for the victorious north, not the defeated south. He recalled the last night with Amos, crouched by a campfire, discussing an incident which had been echoed by the woman he'd earlier encountered. Rebels devoid of ammunition had thrown rocks at a troop of Union soldiers. 'They're fighting for their homes,' Amos had said, 'just as we did when people came to take over the valley of the Tatanka. That's what people do, Charlie, fight to protect their own.'

Charlie couldn't disagree with that but the southerners had fought their war and lost, and that situation couldn't be altered by these isolated attacks. He puzzled over the situation while he rode the seven miles to Pottersville.

# 3

Heading towards Pottersville meant
that Charlie was looping back towards a
trail he'd already travelled. Unwittingly,
he'd passed to the north of the town
earlier that day but as there was
nowhere that he needed to be in a
hurry, he was content to ride along with
the teamsters. Conversation was sparse
and the wagons pulled off in the
direction of some large store-houses
when they reached the first buildings of
the settlement. Charlie rode on towards
the main thoroughfare in search of
stabling for his mount and a room
where he could lay his head for a
couple of nights.

The stableman assured Charlie that
the wound in the horse's flank was
unlikely to develop into anything
serious and that in a day or two it
would be fit enough to carry him again.

As an extra precaution the man offered to treat it with an ointment that he'd smeared on many similar injuries. Content that the horse was in good hands, Charlie went in search of his own billet.

Pottersville was a well-established town, its origin dating back almost a hundred years so that many of the buildings were substantial with firm foundations. The signs affixed to the walls told of its former status as one of the state's major trading centres. Two banks had, at one time, flourished on the main street but now only one was open for business. The other wore the marks of neglect that had become commonplace on Charlie's travels, with peeling paintwork and boards nailed over doors and windows. The bank wasn't the only building on Main Street which had fallen into disuse. The war had forced the closure of a hardware store, a milliner, two eating-houses and a law firm, but it was the biggest derelict building that brought Charlie to a standstill. It was stone-built with a raised platform running its entire length. Carved into the stonework above the door were the words that proclaimed its now redundant purpose: Slave Market.

Charlie paused only for a moment, unwilling to draw attention to himself or for any of the local citizens to see the repulsion he felt for the former function of the building which he suspected showed clearly on his face. Slavery had been at the core of the wealth of which the south was now bereft. He didn't want his behaviour to be interpreted as that of a northerner gloating over the defeat of the south. He moved on, seeing the sign of the Magnolia Hotel further down the street.

Despite the warmth of the day and the fact that stores were still open for business, there were few people on the street. Here and there, bonneted ladies with baskets on their arms paraded the boardwalk and men lounged against posts or chatted without excitement in groups. No one paid heed to Charlie until he approached the long-fronted Wild Horse Saloon. Two men sat on the shaded porch and their conversation ended as Charlie neared. One of the men wore a Confederate grey jacket and sucked on a white claypipe which he held in his right hand. As Charlie drew closer he saw that the left sleeve of the jacket was empty and pinned down to prevent unnecessary flapping.

A pair of crutches were propped against the wall close to where the second man sat. Charlie wondered if that man, too, was an amputee. The price of survival had been great for many. Charlie knew that he was fortunate that he could hide his scars under his shirt and that strangers were unaware of the injuries he'd suffered. For a moment he met the gaze of the one-armed man and for a moment considered speaking, wondered if they would shun him once they realized he was from the north, but the opportunity for conversation was stolen from him in dramatic fashion.

The usual low hum of saloon conversation had reached Charlie as he'd walked along the street but at that moment it erupted into a series of crashes and curses as the swing doors of the Wild Horse were swept aside to their full extent, banging against the building's wooden walls with such violence that the sound they made caused two ladies across the street to react as though guns had been discharged. A figure hurtled through the doorway, landed with a bone-jarring thud then rolled off the boardwalk on to the dusty street close to Charlie's feet. He was a young man, no more than eighteen to Charlie's reckoning, who wore rough riding clothes, a grey derby hat and an ill-fitting gunbelt around his waist. When his hat parted company with his head it revealed unkempt hair not much darker than straw. His face was a mask of anger, narrowed eyes glared hatred and his lips had parted in a scowl. His right hand clutched for the pistol he carried but he didn't complete the movement.

Another man had closely followed him through the doorway but had done so of his own volition. This second person, who had stopped at the edge of the boardwalk so that he could look down on the youth in the dust, paused a second before speaking. Although not above average height he presented a figure of authority, adopting a stance that advertised his dominance of the situation to everyone who had gathered around. His feet were apart, his legs braced like a prize-fighter awaiting his opponent's next attack, and his arms were akimbo, his fists resting on his hips. His hair was thick, black and curled on his forehead and around his ears. He wore a trimmed moustache above his thick lips and dark eyebrows arched over mahogany-coloured eyes.

He raised his hands from his hips and gripped the lapels of a colourful silk waistcoat which he wore over an unfussy white shirt. 'Keep your hand

41

away from that iron, Clint,' he said, making his voice loud so that everyone heard his words. 'This is your last warning. Either keep control of your temper or don't come back here. This is my business and as long as those who come in can pay for what I'm selling they are welcome here. Perhaps you have reason to be aggrieved by the outcome of the war but you are not fighting new battles in here. Until you are man enough to hold your liquor, don't come back.'

For a long moment the man looked down at the boy, making sure that he'd understood the message then turned abruptly, back towards the swing doors that took him into the saloon. Two men, who had watched the scene from the doorway of the Wild Horse, stepped on to the road to stand alongside the youth who had picked himself up from the ground and was busy dusting down his clothes. One of them uttered a low comment which did nothing to pacify the youth and when he set off along the street without them they exchanged amused looks which denoted a tolerance of which they'd grown accustomed.

From his seat on the saloon porch the veteran with one arm spoke loud enough for the youth to hear. 'If he's so keen to fight he should have been with us at Manassas.'

The young man stopped and stared in their direction. His retort, when it came, was heavy with anger and intentionally insulting. 'We might not have lost if I'd been there.'

The veteran scoffed him. 'We didn't lose at Manassas, kid, not either of the battles there. That doesn't mean we want to fight them again, though.'

The two men with the youth hustled him on his way down the street, both of them pouring words into his ears which he didn't want to hear. Charlie watched their progress for a moment then stepped on to the boardwalk and pushed his way into the Wild Horse saloon.

The high counter, like the interior, was L-shaped with tables for customers in both sections. At the far end of the larger area Charlie could see a faro wheel and a piano, although neither of these was currently being played. Most of the customers were in this section, either lounging against the bar with their glasses of beer or whiskey, or assembled in small groups around the dozen or so tables that were placed around the room.

Because the half-dozen tables in the smaller area were covered with red checked cloths, Charlie assumed that that section was reserved for diners. The only occupants at that moment were two young men who were waiting for their food to be served but standing at their table was the man in the colourful waistcoat. As Charlie stepped forward he overheard their conversation.

'The war will never be over if hot-heads like young Clint try to pick a fight with everyone they meet from the north.'

'We're not looking for trouble,' said one of the men, a lanky fellow in a rough cotton shirt.

'Do you mean to stay long in Pottersville?'

'Just passing through, we'll be moving on tomorrow or the next day.'

'Heading north?' asked the saloon man. 'Going home?'

It was the other traveller who replied. He was a couple of years younger than his companion and his words were accompanied by a ready grin which made him crinkle his eyes when he spoke. 'Not yet,' he said. 'We heard there might be work south of here, in the timberlands. Our brother is already working down there.'

The lanky brother dropped his gaze to the floor and Charlie suspected that he thought his sibling's tongue was looser than the situation demanded but when he looked up again he grinned and said, 'It'll be some reunion when we meet up.'

'I'm sure it will,' said the man in the

waistcoat. 'Your food will be here soon.' To Charlie, who was making his way to the counter at the side of the room, he asked, 'Can I help you?'

'You can if there's more food where you are fetching theirs from.'

Assured that there was enough to feed him too, Charlie ordered a beer while he waited for it to arrive. The man introduced himself as Mort Goudry, the owner of the Wild Horse which he claimed was the best saloon in Pottersville and where a traveller would find good food, beer, gambling games and girls.

Charlie claimed the table next to the one at which the brothers were sitting. He introduced himself and learned that the brothers were called Henry and Dave Willis. 'Didn't mean to overhear your conversation,' he told them, 'but out on the street that fellow seemed to be quelling the antics of a young troublemaker.'

'It weren't nothing,' said Henry, the older brother.

Dave, the younger but more talkative brother, chipped in a few more words. 'Perhaps he'd had too much to drink. He seemed keen to pick a fight with us but no one else backed his play.'

'The surrender hurt a lot of people down here,' Charlie said. 'I ran into a bit of trouble south of town earlier in the day.'

'We're heading south,' Dave told him.

Charlie explained that his confrontation with the woman at the farm had taken place some miles to the west of the trail. 'Keep to the trail and you won't go near her place.' He placed his hand over his holster and spoke again. 'First opportunity, I aim to cut the flap off this.'

'Ought to get another,' said Dave, and he rose to his feet to allow Charlie to see the gun-rig he was wearing. Clearly, it was a new purchase. The brown leather was decorated with a distinctive filigree pattern. 'What do you think of this?' he asked proudly.

Charlie had to agree it was a fine piece of work. 'I was only suggesting that you approach strangers carefully until you know how friendly they're likely to be.'

'Sound advice, Charlie,' said Henry Willis. 'Perhaps we all should have gone back north when the war ended.'

'I don't want to return home empty-handed,' Charlie told the brothers, 'but I haven't found any way to make a fortune. As soon as my horse is rested I'm heading for the timberlands, too.'

The brothers exchanged a swift look but their meal arrived thereby ending the conversation and, Charlie suspected, the brief association, too.

After eating, Charlie went in search of a room and found it in a house run by a widow. Any curiosity she entertained about his recent past she kept to herself. If she and the stableman were typical of Pottersville residents then there was no place for war-time bias when striving for renewed prosperity.

48

The need for revenue outweighed a defeated political ideal. The room was small but the bed was firm. After washing and changing his shirt he left the house and returned to Main Street.

Outside the first saloon he reached a number of coal oil lamps had been hung on nails hammered into walls and support posts to attract men to the pleasures that waited within. It was a tactic that reaped dividends because the room was crowded. Consequently, Charlie's entrance went unnoticed by most people and even the bartender displayed little interest in the tall stranger once he'd handed over the necessary coins to pay for his drinks.

After a while, Charlie took a place at a table where a poker game was in progress. The other four players were local men who barely introduced themselves but didn't spend time quizzing him, either. They played seriously but chatted in the sort of mocking manner that is peculiar to close friends. It reminded Charlie of the many hours he, Amos and Fess Salter had spent in similar fashion, squatted in front of their camp tents waiting for orders to move. For a few moments he felt more relaxed than at any time since leaving his home in the valley of the Tatanka River.

Hence, it took a few moments for him to realize that the noise level in the saloon had on the one hand increased and yet on the other had taken on a hushed quality. Two of his fellow card players were looking over his head to some sort of commotion at the other end of the room where a high, youthful voice piqued with anger and alcohol was raised above all others. His tirade had brought an end to many of the conversations that had, until that moment, filled the room. Charlie twisted in his seat, struggled to catch a glimpse of the man who was causing the disturbance.

One of the card players passed on the information. 'Clint Revlon,' he said, his voice low but carrying an inflection that told Charlie that the name would not be a surprise to any of the other three. Indeed, Charlie, too, had vaguely identified the voice as one he'd heard earlier that day and swiftly identified the young man that Mort Goudry had faced down outside the Wild Horse saloon.

Clint Revlon's goading voice now filled the saloon, his curses and threats directed with venom at two men who had their backs to Charlie. Clint Revlon, face flushed and hat pushed to the back of his head, had adopted a gunman's stance. His shoulders were slightly forward and his right arm was bent so that the hand was merely inches from the walnut handle of the pistol in its cut-away holster.

Behind him, one of the card players spoke. 'That kid'll bring the army down on us if he isn't checked.'

Charlie turned back to see which of the men had spoken but another of the players was pushing back his chair and rising to his feet. When he adjusted his jacket Charlie saw a portion of a lawman's badge attached to the shirt below. The man wiped his hand over his moustache and walked forward.

'Clint Revlon,' he called when he was yet twenty paces from the youth, 'if your hand goes any closer to that pistol I'll blow you out of your boots.'

Bystanders scuttled aside to give the sheriff a clear path to the incident. Clint Revlon seemed startled by the lawman's sudden appearance.

'What's the argument about?' The sheriff's first question was directed at Clint but it was quickly followed by another for the two men being harangued by the youth. 'Who are you?' he asked.

'I'm Henry Willis. This is my brother Dave. We're not causing any trouble, sheriff.'

'They are northern soldiers.' Clint spat out the words. 'Causing trouble is their business. Killers, murderers and thieves every one.'

'Clint, I know your father and

brother were killed fighting for the Confederacy but so were a lot of other people. The war is lost. Now we've got to build for the future. If people like you are left unchecked then the army will impose martial law here. That's something that neither I nor the majority of people want, so this is the last warning I intend to give you. If you continue to cause disruptions in this way I'll have to put you in jail. There's been one complaint about your behaviour already today so I want you to give me that gun then get on your horse and leave town. Don't come back until you can control yourself.' The sheriff held out his hand for the weapon.

Clint Revlon's face, already flushed with alcohol, deepened with colour. 'I'm not handing over my gun,' he said, his defiance raising a murmur of disbelief from those gathered around. 'If you think you can take it, sheriff, you're welcome to try.'

The sheriff reacted with the speed of a rattlesnake. His left hand reached out and gripped Clint's right to prevent him from reaching for the gun while with the open palm of his right hand he slapped Clint hard across the left cheek, forcing him to stumble to his right. He backhanded him across the right cheek, jerking his head in the opposite direction, repeated the dose then thrust him hard against the high counter, using force enough to have done damage to his ribs or spine.

'If you ever speak to me like that again your ma will be attending your funeral. Now give me that gun.' This time the sheriff didn't wait for Clint to comply, simply pulled it from the holster and laid it on the counter. 'Now I'm going to put you on your horse and chase you out of town. And my previous order still stands: don't come back until you've grown up.'

Grabbing a handful of Clint's shirt, the sheriff pulled the shamed youth to the door. He struggled little but he threw a look in the direction of the Willis brothers which, to those who witnessed it, made it clear that he held them responsible for the humiliation.

Nonetheless, moments later the sound of a horse hastily leaving town reached the ears of those in the saloon where the noise was still below its usual raucous level. The sheriff returned to his interrupted poker game but Charlie Jefferson decided to quit his hand and approached the Willis boys.

'Reckon we're unwelcome in this town,' Dave told him.

'It's only one man causing you trouble,' Charlie said, 'and he's banished.'

'Even so,' said Henry, 'he's a local fellow and bound to have friends here in Pottersville. We don't want to spark off some sort of vendetta so we'll be on our way in the morning.'

'Good luck,' said Charlie. 'Perhaps we'll meet up again down south.'

Charlie walked out of the saloon into the dark, warm night. With the help of the lamps that were lit here and there along the street, he strode towards the Wild Horse Saloon, figuring he'd find out what entertainment it had to offer before returning to his boarding room. Few people were on the street, occasionally he'd see a distant figure crossing from one side to the other before disappearing through a bar-room's doors.

There were no lamps lit outside the Wild Horse but there was sufficient noise coming from within to assure Charlie that this was a livelier spot than the saloon he'd recently departed. Someone was thumping out 'Sweet Betsy from Pike' on the piano and the words were being sung by a female voice which was too coarse to be pleasant. Charlie regarded the now empty seats that had been occupied earlier by the wounded veterans and chose to sit there until the woman had finished murdering the song.

He'd been sitting in the darkness for three or four minutes, his quirly smouldering down to his knuckles, when a scraping sound carried from across the street. He peered into the gloom of the gap between the buildings opposite, one of which was a merchant's store and the other the office of a lawyer. There was no immediate repetition of the noise so Charlie assumed it was a dog or perhaps a racoon or some other adventurous wild scavenger searching among the merchant's debris and waste. Still sitting and with as little fuss as possible, he took a last draw from the burning tobacco then crushed the end under his foot.

Along the street, following in his footsteps, two men approached. They were in conversation, careless, it seemed, of all else around them. Charlie watched them, growing more sure with each step they took that they were the Willis brothers. They were in the centre of the street, the moonlight illuminating them so that they were as clear to see as players on a stage. Charlie began to rise, thinking to call a greeting, but again a sound carried from the alley across the street. The sound was as familiar to Charlie as that of a horse on the run or a bugle at daybreak; it was the working of the mechanism of a repeating rifle. Someone was preparing to fire at the unsuspecting brothers.

'Hey!' Charlie yelled, dragging at the flap that covered the holster that held his pistol.

The rifle fired and Charlie heard the bullet thud into timber somewhere down the street. The Willis boys had dropped to the ground but Charlie didn't think that either had been hit. Before he could draw his gun, the rifle fired again. This time the bullet kicked into the ground close to the brothers but again failed to find its target. Charlie fired across into the space between the two buildings and a ruckus ensued as the shooter, scurrying away from his position, crashed into some of the empty containers left there by the merchant.

Charlie ran forward, fired again and

at the same time called to the two men still lying in the street. Assured by Henry that they had not been hit, Charlie set off to pursue the shooter. At the mouth of the alley another shot was fired throwing splinters from the corner stanchion of the lawyer's office. Charlie withdrew and when he risked another look the gunman had run off. Cautiously, Charlie made his way between the buildings but before he reached the far end he heard someone yelling instructions to a horse and then the beast running off into the darkness of the night.

The gunshots had brought men from the saloons but no one else had witnessed the attempted ambush. Slightly breathless, the sheriff arrived and his mouth tightened when he recognized the intended targets. 'Did you see who it was?' he asked but knew there was only one suspect.

'No,' conceded Charlie, 'but I found this in the alley.' He held up a piece of red material.

The sheriff examined it, unfurled it to reveal what looked like a small sack, but holes had been cut into it so that if pulled over a head it would allow the wearer to see and breathe. Sheriff Brand immediately knew its significance.

'Red Masks,' he muttered.

# 4

Although there were many people in Arkansas, Missouri and Mississippi who retained empathy with the renegade bands and believed that they fought for the honour of the south, few people wanted them to continue the war in their neighbourhood. Despite propaganda which insisted that their targets were carpetbaggers and those civic leaders, landowners and people of influence who showed favour to the northern interlopers, the fact was that people had been killed without discrimination and the property of innocent people destroyed. It was known that many of the riders in these renegade bands had been guerrilla fighters during the war and had served under such leaders as William Quantrill and 'Bloody Bill' Anderson who had adopted a creed of bloody violence. Among the worst of the renegade bands that creed still prevailed.

One of the worst bands was known as the Red Masks because of the red cotton hoods they wore during raids; such a hood as that which Charlie Jefferson had found in the alley. Its discovery galvanized Sheriff Bland into action. Southern sympathies set aside, the town leaders of Pottersville had agreed that the future prosperity of their town lay in attracting new businesses and if that meant accepting northern investment then that was what they would do. They had taken into consideration the activities of the renegade bands and knew that until such time as they were rounded up by the army, that policy made them a possible target. Accordingly, plans had been drawn up to defend the town in the event of an attack and Sheriff Bland now set them in motion.

At critical points on every street, barricades were constructed. In the first instance, wagons were drawn across the street then loaded with barrels, boxes, timber and anything that added height and provided extra cover for the defenders. Those citizens who had been identified as likely targets for the renegades were informed and advised to attend to their own defence. To no avail, Mayor Darwin urged the sheriff to send for military backup.

'Fort Smith is more than a hundred miles away,' Sheriff Bland told him. 'If the Red Masks attack it will be over long before any soldiers are able to reach us.' Sheriff Bland didn't add that he was reluctant to bring the military to Pottersville because once a foothold was established it would be difficult to get rid of them. Policing Pottersville was his responsibility and he wasn't going to declare himself incompetent to any blue-coat commander.

All the men of the town were summoned to man the barricades. Together with Henry and Dave Willis, Charlie Jefferson joined them. All night they waited, watching and listening, checking and rechecking their weapons, but when dawn's first pink light hit the roof of the court house they knew that their vigil had been in vain. Finding the red hood had triggered a false alarm, Pottersville had not been the target of the Red Masks but the attempted murder of the Willis brothers had probably been the work of a member of that renegade band. All that remained was for the barricades to be removed so that the town could prepare for another day of business as best as it was able.

Confirmation that the Red Masks had not intended to raid Pottersville came via a telegraph message to Mayor Darwin from his counterpart in Pine Bluff sixty miles to the east. The first message was short of information, nothing more than an announcement that that town had been attacked by the renegades, but as the day wore on more details emerged and it became clear that people had been killed and

buildings destroyed. Burning and loot-
ing had occurred on a massive scale
and the raiders had stolen a great
amount of money from the bank.
Although the raiders had escaped
without any known casualties, a troop
of soldiers who had been in the vicinity
were now on their heels with orders to
pursue until caught.

Henry and Dave Willis found Charlie
enjoying breakfast in a coffee house on
Main Street. They expressed the opinion that last night's shooter was
probably the same young fellow who
had tried to goad them into a fight
earlier in the evening and, that being
the case, there was nothing to be gained
by hanging around to let him have
another go.

'The sheriff chased him out of town,'
Charlie said. 'Perhaps he hung around
to have another try but I don't think
he'll come back again in a hurry.'

'Perhaps not,' replied Henry, 'but
we've got no proof that it was the same
person and if not how long will it be

before someone else with a grudge against the north is successful?'

'We're quitting this place,' said Dave. 'We'd like it if you came with us.'

'That's right,' his brother said, 'we owe you for what you did last night. If you hadn't shouted a warning we might be dead.'

Charlie dismissed the notion that they were in his debt. He would have interfered against an ambusher no matter who the victim.

Dave spoke again, keeping his voice low, keeping his words from the ears of the people in the room. 'Like you, we're heading for the timberland but we mean to make a detour on the way.'

Henry, the older brother, took charge of the conversation. 'Our brother John is working at a lumber camp. According to him every site down there has grown because of the demands of rebuilding since the end of the war. In his letters he complains of a shortage of good food and reckons that the workers would pay well for good beef steaks.

Across the border, in Texas, cattle roam wild. We're thinking of driving some of them down to the timberland. Perhaps a hundred head at first in case John's diagnosis is wrong. But we'll do the slaughtering and cooking so that everything will be profit. If the scheme is a success we'll repeat the process.'

'If you join us we'll be able to drive a bigger herd,' Dave interjected. 'We'll split the profits in equal parts. You said you wanted to make a fortune and this should earn you more than working at a lumber mill.'

The offer took Charlie by surprise and he tried swiftly to assess its worth. For an instant the face of Ruth Prescott filled his imagination and the desire to return to her and the valley of the Tatanka River was overpowering. Dave was right, what the brothers planned would surely generate considerably more money than labouring, and serving up steaks would also be more profitable than selling the beeves at eight dollars a head to some other camp cook. The only down side to the enterprise was Texas. That state was in turmoil, politically split between those who were opposed to seeking re-entry to the Union but further divided by those who were working for it to become once more a separate republic. That political chaos had led to lawlessness on a grand scale and Charlie guessed that people driving Texas cattle, mavericks though they may be, over state boundaries would be considered rustlers. It was a risk, but Charlie knew there was no profit without it.

'I guess you've got a partner,' he told them.

The immediate drawback to the scheme was that the brothers wanted to leave Pottersville that day while Charlie was anxious to give his mount another day of rest. The man at the livery stable offered to resolve the impasse by taking Charlie's mount in exchange for a roan gelding he kept in a stall at the rear of the stable. The stableman's eagerness suggested to Charlie that he would be getting the worst part of the deal and although his inspection of the livery beast showed no obvious defect it looked disinterested and lazy. A speedy animal wasn't necessary but if he was going to be hustling cows across the territory it was important that the beast had stamina and agility. Consequently, he chose to wait another day but the brothers rode off mid-afternoon promising to wait for Charlie at the Ouachita River eighteen miles south of the town. When they were re-united they would cut west for Texas.

* * *

Next day, with the horse's wound almost invisible, Charlie saddled up and quit Pottersville. He touched the brim of his hat as he passed Sheriff Bland who was sitting on the porch outside his office and Charlie sensed an element of relief in the lawman's expression, as though he held Charlie and the Willis brothers responsible for yesterday's violent incidents.

Charlie didn't demand too much of the horse, allowed it to pick its own pace so that he could judge its fitness. It was soon evident that the animal was in good spirits and was moving freely and quickly along the trail. It was about noon when Charlie figured he should be close to the river. He had encountered no other travellers during the morning but now, as he approached a ridge, dust was circling in the air as though a host of riders were gathered beyond. Slowing the horse to walking pace he neared the lip with caution.

The Ouachita River lay below, perhaps fifty feet wide but with hardly enough depth for the horses that were in it to cause a splash. There were four of them, two walking slowly upstream, the others walking downstream. The riders wore the blue blouses of Union soldiers and they matched those of the other twenty men assembled on the bank below Charlie. Some of those soldiers remained in the saddle but a handful had dismounted and were gathered together to inspect something on the ground.

Charlie dismounted and watched from the top of the ridge, waited for them to move on because there was no indication that they meant to make camp at that spot. Whatever their mission it didn't concern him. At least, it didn't concern him until he turned and found himself the object of the attention of three soldiers. They were mounted, a sergeant and two troopers, and how they had approached so quietly was a mystery to Charlie. The troopers' rifles were pointed at him. The sergeant asked the questions, wanted to know his name and business.

'Going south,' Charlie told him, 'looking for work.' The sergeant seemed unconvinced that Charlie was speaking the truth, but when he added, 'I'd arranged to meet a couple of friends near here,' the sergeant's attitude changed.

'You'd better come and join us. Captain Jessop will want to speak to you.' The sergeant led the way and the troopers fell in behind so that Charlie had little choice but to obey.

Captain Jessop watched the arrival of the four horsemen with a stern expression. His hair was dark and his mutton-chop side whiskers were united by a long moustache. His unblinking eyes were small, portending a mean or cruel nature. His voice, when he spoke, was military crisp and expected an immediate response. 'Who is this?' he asked the sergeant almost before the horses had been pulled to a halt.

'Says he's heading south, Captain. Expected to meet a couple of friends here.'

There was a pause before the officer spoke again. 'I'm Captain Jessop,' he announced, 'and you are?'

'Charlie Jefferson.'

'Step down, Charlie Jefferson, and follow me.'

Intrigued by the officer's abrupt

invitation, Charlie dismounted and followed Captain Jessop to the group of soldiers who had formed a rough circle. He was yet eight yards from the men when he saw the boots and realized that a body lay on the ground. As the men parted to admit the officer to the scene, Charlie saw that there were two bodies and instantly recognized the clothing even though the shirts of both men were covered with congealing blood. He began to count the number of bullet wounds in each man then turned away, angry at such needless violence. Their saddles and blankets remained on the ground making it clear that the brothers had been attacked while they slept. There was no sign of their horses or weapons. Henry's empty holster lay on the ground but Dave's fancy new rig had been taken by his killer.

'Henry and Dave Willis,' he told Captain Jessop. 'Do you know who did this?'

'It might have been renegades,' the officer replied, 'although why they would stop to inflict such punishment on these two men is hard to understand. They've been tortured, or at least their death wasn't quick. They have been beaten and suffered gunshot wounds in their arms and legs whose only purpose must have been to cause pain.'

'Are you chasing Red Masks?' asked Charlie.

Captain Jessop regarded Charlie with suspicion, as though information had been disclosed that would undermine the entire military strategy of the Union.

'Their raid at Pine Bluff is the talk of Pottersville,' Charlie told him and went on to explain how Pottersville had considered itself under threat.

Mollified by Charlie's words, Captain Jessop confirmed that his troop were indeed chasing the Red Masks. 'They'll be made to pay for these atrocities as well as those at Pine Bluff,' he declared.

A burial detail was assembled and, while the men were busy digging high on the bank, a rider came galloping from the east. He wore a wide-brimmed prairie hat, decorated with a leather thong around its low, flat-topped crown; his blue shirt was woollen and laced at the throat with a criss-crossing leather strip and his trousers were hard-wearing denim tucked inside brown, calf-high boots. Across his saddle he carried his unsheathed rifle. He reined his horse to a halt in front of the officer.

'What news?' asked Captain Jessop. 'Have you found a trail?'

The man spat from the saddle with such emphasis that the negative reply was barely worth uttering.

'I covered a whole circle and found nothing. I'm thinking they've travelled along the river from here,' he said. He looked first upstream then downstream then spat again. 'It'll take time to pick up their tracks.'

'We'll camp here an hour while we figure out what to do next,' said Captain Jessop. 'That'll give us time to complete the burials, partake of rations and refresh the horses.'

The man began to step down from the saddle just as Charlie Jefferson approached. 'Fess,' he called, 'Fess Salter, is that you?'

'Charlie Jefferson!'

'Do you know this man?' asked Captain Jessop.

'Why sure,' replied Fess. 'We fought side by side for two years. What are you doing this far south, Charlie?'

'You were right about Petersburg,' he said, 'it was the wrong place for making a fortune.'

'And you're heading for the right place now?'

Charlie shook his head. 'I doubt it, Fess.' He explained his association with the two dead men and confessed that now he had to fall back on finding work at a lumber camp.

'I thought you'd be at the far end of the Oregon Trail by this time,' he said to Fess.

'I would have been if I hadn't run

into Colonel Crook again. He was at Fort Smith when I rode through and he persuaded me to act as scout for the army. You can see for yourself that these renegades need to be stopped, Charlie. Most people are looking to the future and trying to rebuild their lives after the war. These men aren't helping anyone or fighting for anything but their own gain. Eventually, those people who are aiding them will realize their mistake, but a lot of killing and damage might be done in the meanwhile. They've killed your friends, Charlie. Doesn't that make you want to put a stop to their raids?'

It did. He hadn't known the Willis boys long and didn't know them well but he did know that their killing could not have brought gain to anyone. They were just two drifters looking to keep out of trouble and earn a reasonably honest dollar. Whoever had killed them had brutalized them unnecessarily. Charlie was eager to know who had done it and why.

# 5

There had been something about Dave Willis that had reminded Charlie Jefferson of Amos Prescott — not anything physical, not the colour of hair nor the shape of the face nor the manner of walking. It showed in the eagerness with which they had both approached life, the chatter and ever-ready smile that offered friendliness first to each new face they met. On several occasions Charlie had accused Amos of naivety, thrown him a look of caution similar to that which Henry Willis had thrown his younger brother when he believed he was talking too freely, but they were men with whom it was impossible to remain angry. They expected others to be as just and undemanding as themselves.

Now they were both dead and the senseless killing of the Willis brothers angered Charlie. It also took from him the opportunity to make money by driving Texas cattle to the lumber camps in southern Arkansas. Any continuation of that plan floundered on his need to find partners prepared to run the risk of chasing cattle out of Texas and a cook to serve up the steaks at the lumber camp. After the first raid it had been agreed that Dave would prepare the meals while Charlie and Henry brought more stock from Texas.

So, when Fess Salter suggested that he throw in his lot with the army to capture the renegades that were becoming more daring and more violent in their escapades to disrupt reconstruction of the state, Charlie agreed. After the burial of the brothers he discarded his military holster and wrapped Henry's old gunbelt around his waist. Then, while the soldiers ate their rations, he and Fess rode the river to try to pick up the trail of the renegades.

Charlie rode up-river, keeping to the centre of the water course so that he could check both banks for any sign that the band had passed that way. Fess had estimated a force two dozen strong, the trail of so many horsemen would be difficult to obscure completely. However, after covering more than two miles, his scouting proved fruitless so he returned to the bivouac point in the hope that Fess had been more successful.

The soldiers were resaddling their mounts ready to move out when he got back.

'We've lost them,' Fess grumbled to Captain Jessop. 'My hunch is they've ridden along this stream,' he added, 'we need to go farther.'

'In which direction?' asked the officer.

'I'd be guessing whichever way I picked.'

'Then we'll have to abandon the pursuit. We haven't the provisions to continue any longer. We'll return to the temporary base at Benton and consider our next manoeuvre.'

The twist of Fess's face showed his reluctance to give up the mission. 'If it's all right with you, Captain, Charlie and me will search a bit longer. Perhaps we'll find a trail or some clue that'll lead us to them.'

Captain Jessop had no objection so the two civilians hung back when the troop rode away.

'They are around here somewhere, Charlie,' said Fess. 'We've been on their heels for a day and a half and when we've got close to them they've changed direction or picked up the pace and tried to leave us behind, but this is the first time they've pulled a stunt to hide their trail.'

'Meaning?'

'Meaning they are close to their hideout and they don't want to lead us to it.'

Charlie acknowledged his friend's logic. 'Have you got a plan for finding them?'

'No. Either we stick together and hope we pick the right direction to search or we split up and meet back here at nightfall.'

'Perhaps there's another way,' said Charlie, and proceeded to tell Fess about the events in Pottersville. 'If that red mask belonged to Clint Revlon we may be able to trace this gang of bushwhackers through him.'

★  ★  ★

They rode into Pottersville separately, figuring there was no reason to let folks know they were associated. Charlie hitched his horse at the rail outside the sheriff's office and stepped inside the small building. Sheriff Bland's expression registered his surprise.

'Didn't expect to see you again so soon.'

'There were soldiers at the river searching for the Red Masks who raided Pine Bluff. What they found were the bodies of the Willis brothers.'

Sheriff Bland cursed. 'Fate decreed that those boys would die here.'

'Fate or Clint Revlon,' said Charlie.

'Clint?'

'Sure. Either he followed them when they left town or he's one of the Red Masks and they were unfortunate enough to cross his path out by the Ouachita.'

Bland shook his head, slowly, a man trying to nudge thoughts into alignment. 'He's a wild one,' he said, 'but young. I don't know how he'd get mixed up with bushwhacker gangs. No one here in Pottersville has that sort of reputation.'

'Where do you suppose he went when you chased him out of town?' asked Charlie.

'His family home is south and west of here.' Sheriff Bland's voice was low, as though he wasn't sure he wanted Charlie to hear the words, 'but I figured he'd head for Hot Springs. He bellies up to the Cotton Queen Bar in Hot Springs when he's not making life tough for Mort Goudry here at the Wild Horse.'

Charlie stored the names in his memory and took his leave of the lawman then led his horse to the livery for a feed. In an hour he'd meet up with Fess outside town to share any information they'd gathered.

★ ★ ★

Trusting in Charlie's version of events two nights earlier, and therefore certain that Clint Revlon was no longer in Pottersville, Fess Salter dropped his name to the barman who served him a beer in the Wild Horse. Fess swallowed two mouthfuls of beer, put down the glass then wiped his sleeve across his mouth. He grinned, as though he'd just fulfilled a long awaited pleasure. 'Good,' he said. 'Clint told me the beer here was always cold and refreshing.'

'Clint?' queried the barman.

'Yeah. Clint Revlon told me I'd find him here.'

The barman shook his head and glanced at two fellows lounging nearby.

'Clint's out of town. Don't expect him back in a hurry.'

Fess grunted as though the barman's words formed the worst news he could have been given. 'Told me he could find some work for me if I needed it. And I need it.'

'Didn't know the kid was intending to rebuild his property. The family farm is south and west of here but I'm not sure you'll find him there, either.'

Once more the expression on Fess's face showed amusement but this time its message was less of pleasure, more mercenary and sinister. 'I'm not sure that farming was the job on offer.'

Fess lifted his glass again and the barman drifted away to serve customers at the other end of the room. While he drank, Fess allowed his gaze to take in the two men nearest. He was sure they were using the mirror behind the bar to study him. When he'd drained his glass he called to the barman for a refill.

'Are any of Clint's friends in tonight?' Fess looked over his shoulder at the busy tables.

'He doesn't have many of those around here at present. Got on the wrong side of the sheriff a couple of nights ago and left town. How do you know him?'

'Met him in a saloon in Pine Bluff a couple of weeks ago and pulled him out of a scrape with a saloon keeper. Boy, had he stored a load of whiskey behind his belt. Ha! He was raising quite a ruckus about carpetbaggers and jay-hawker bands that are making life difficult around here. He'd have ended up in the sheriff's cells if I hadn't got him out of there and into an eating place where he could get some solid food into his belly.'

'Why did you do that?'

Fess raised his glass again and drank. 'Suppose I liked the fact that his southern spirit hadn't been destroyed by the surrender, but bar-room brawling isn't going to get him anywhere. As it turned out it seemed that my good deed would have some reward. He promised to find work for me if I looked him up in Pottersville.'

The two men near Fess picked up their glasses and moved to the far end of the counter, showing an interest in the card games that were being played at the various tables as they passed. When they stopped it was to take up the same lounging posture they'd previously held. The barman too, moved away, tending to business. Fess looked around the room but no one seemed interested in his presence. He had hoped that the story he'd spun would spread throughout the room and raise enough interest to draw out someone who knew Clint Revlon, but no one approached him so, when his glass was empty, he decided to try again in another saloon.

'Mister.' The barman stood directly behind him at the other side of the counter. 'You might try Delaney's Bar down the street. A fellow called Brad Jones is in there. He's a pal of Clint

Revlon and might know where he is now.'

'Obliged for the information,' he said, tipped his hat and pushed his way towards the exit.

The street was dark and Fess paused on the boardwalk wondering what Charlie had learned from the sheriff. Lamps illuminated several buildings on both sides of the street but Fess headed left which had been the direction the barman had indicated. His boots made a solid sound on the wood planks as he walked on. Across the street there was a light in the sheriff's office but he didn't interrupt his stride; he and Charlie had agreed not to make contact with each other until they were once more beyond the town limits.

Ahead, almost in the centre of the street, the building line was interrupted. The blacksmith's forge and the hay provender store were set back and fronted by a corral in which the blacksmith's customers left their beasts while awaiting his service. Across the street from the corral was a low, single-storey establishment from which fiddle and accordion music leaked. In the darkness it wasn't possible for Fess to read the name board that was fixed on the wall above the door but, as he got nearer, the smoky lamps that hung on the wall cast enough light for him to be able to read the letters that formed a semi-circle in the window. Delaney's Bar. As he turned to cross the street a sound behind him had him reaching for his gun.

'Easy, mister,' a voice hissed. 'Keep your hand away from your gun. We sent the message to bring you down to Delaney's.'

Fess turned, slowly, keeping his hand clear of the butt of his pistol but still wary of the intent of those in the shadows behind. Two men stepped clear of the alley in which they had been waiting. It took less than a moment for Fess to recognize them as the two who had been close at hand when he'd told his tale to the barman.

Their pistols were drawn and pointed at Fess.

'Brad Jones?' asked Fess.

The man chuckled. 'Don't know anybody with that name but it sure got you down here in a hurry.'

'What do you want?'

'I'm interested in that tale you told about Clint Revlon.'

'Do you know Clint?'

'I know him. Don't recall any time he visited Pine Bluff.'

'Are you his guardian?'

'Not exactly.'

'What does that mean? I figured he was old enough to travel about on his own. Had his own horse and everything when I met him.'

'Yeah,' the man said, 'he likes to think he's a man but his mouth runs like a righteous woman's. No accounting for the amount of nonsense that comes out.'

'I can't argue that he'd had his fill of liquor that day but he spoke up for the south with more passion than I've heard since Lee signed the surrender.'

'Did you fight in the war?'

'I did.'

'You mind telling me on which side? Your speech isn't exactly that of a southern gentleman.'

'It isn't that of a northern carpetbagger either. I'm from the west. Fought my first battle at Glorieta Pass in '62.' Fess wasn't surprised by the uncomprehending look exchanged by the men, the Battle at Glorieta Pass had been fought in the west when the Confederacy had hoped to recruit California to its cause. 'That was part of General Sibley's campaign in New Mexico,' he told them.

Realizing that that was a part of the war with which they had little knowledge, the spokesman of the two men turned the conversation back to Clint Revlon. 'What kind of work did the kid promise you?'

'He wasn't specific, just said that he could put me in the way of something profitable that would strike a blow for the south. I'm not sure what he had in mind but like I told the bartender, I'm not expecting it to involve fixing fences or milking cows.'

The two men shared another silent look, as though coming to a decision that neither felt capable of making.

'Where's your horse?' asked the talker.

Fess pointed back to where he'd come from. 'Outside the saloon.'

'OK. We're on our way to meet up with Clint. You can come with us.'

'Sure,' he replied, 'can you put up your weapons now?'

With a show of reluctance, the men did so. 'Tom,' the speaker spoke to his partner, 'you go with him. I'll collect our horses from the livery.' Fess thought that the words were accompanied by a significant head movement, an additional instruction, but in the darkness he couldn't be certain that a signal had been given. Indeed, he was wrestling with the problem of getting his own message to Charlie Jefferson. It seemed that they were to leave town immediately and he had no idea in which direction they would travel.

'Where are we going?' he asked.

'Hot Springs.'

Tom and Fess returned to the boardwalk of the Wild Horse Saloon where Fess checked the cinch while waiting for the arrival of the other man with the horses. When they saw him approaching through the darkness, Tom said he had to let Lily Rose know that he couldn't keep their appointment and stepped inside the saloon.

For a brief moment, Fess considered climbing into the saddle and riding hard out of Pottersville, but he knew that he was in the very position that he had hoped to be in. The fact that he wasn't sure that the two men believed his story and that perhaps they planned to kill him when they were well away from the town was a hazard he had accepted when he'd chosen to ride once more for Colonel Crook. If he'd been able to get a message to Charlie

Jefferson he'd have ridden away secure in the knowledge that his back was covered, but Charlie was nowhere to be seen and now, as the talker with the horses approached and Tom pushed aside the swing doors to step on to the boardwalk the last chance seemed to have passed him by.

'Mount up,' commanded the man as he threw the reins to Tom. 'And you,' he told Fess.

'The name's Fess,' he said, 'it might be handy to introduce ourselves since we're going to be travelling together.'

'He's Tom and I'm Wade,' said the mounted man. 'Now, let's ride.'

# 6

Wade's visit to the livery stable wasn't restricted to collecting the horses.

'Get a message to the boss,' he told the night hostler. 'Tell him we're taking this stranger to Hot Springs. If his story doesn't check out with Clint Revlon we'll deal with him.' After a pause, he added, 'Perhaps we'll question him again when we're on the trail. If we don't like what he says he'll never get to Hot Springs.'

The hostler, a short man with a hawkish, grey-skinned face, flashed a warning look to Wade and tilted his head towards the inner reaches of the stable where a figure could be seen tending to one of the animals. The man was a stranger to Wade and, by the manner in which he went about his business, was paying no attention to what passed between him and the stableman. Even so, Wade spoke no more and was assured by the hostler's curt head movement that his message would be delivered at the earliest opportunity.

There was no reason why Wade should recognize Charlie Jefferson — only once and for merely a matter of moments had they been in the same vicinity — but Charlie remembered Wade as one of the men who had led Clint Revlon away from the Wild Horse Saloon when he'd been ejected by Mort Goudry. Not wanting to draw attention to himself, Charlie had continued with the administrations to his horse and pretended total disinterest in the activity towards the front of the stable. Although Wade had spoken below a normal conversation level, enough words had reached Charlie's ears to convince him that Fess Salter had successfully caught the attention of Clint's friends but that he was now in danger.

Charlie had a decision to make. He'd

clearly heard the instruction to the stableman and if 'the boss' was the leader of the Red Masks then discovering his identity could be decisive in ending their raids, but more importantly, Fess was in peril and needed his immediate assistance. So, no sooner had Wade ridden away from the livery than Charlie set to work saddling his own animal. The horse had been fed but, on his orders, only a small portion of a standard meal. Whilst not confident that their ruse would lead them to Clint Revlon, Charlie and Fess were, none-theless, anxious to be prepared to pursue their quarry without delay. Consequently, neither they nor their horses would be overfed until they'd found their man.

Figuring that Wade and his cohort would not confront Fess until they were well clear of Pottersville, Charlie saw little reason for drawing attention to his own departure by tearing out of town in pursuit. Hot Springs lay thirty-five miles due west of Pottersville with rough, rocky land between. Charlie saw no reason why they wouldn't stick to the recognized trail so he travelled at little more than a canter, cautiously, so that the sound of his horse's hoof-beats didn't carry ahead and warn them that someone was on their trail.

*　*　*

Seven miles were covered at an easy lope before Wade raised his arm and, having gained the attention of the other two, led them away from the trail and into a treeless, basin-like recess where the darkness made it almost impossible to see each other. Fess was in no doubt that this was a pre-arranged halt, the certainty with which Wade guided them made it clear that he knew of it in advance. When Wade rode ahead, Tom circled his horse so that he would be at the rear of the threesome. It was a slick manoeuvre and Fess now had one man in front and one behind. His level of watchfulness increased and his right hand rested on his thigh close to the handle of his revolver.

'Why are we stopping?' he asked.

'There's no hurry,' Wade told him, 'and our horses have been ridden hard over the past couple of days.'

'Don't understand why you rushed to leave Pottersville if that is the case. Could still be drinking cold beer in a saloon rather than eating trail dust. Finding Clint Revlon would keep another day.'

'Sure it would,' said Wade, 'but sometimes it's better to travel at night to escape prying eyes. In our business we don't always want people to know when we leave one town or reach another.'

'I don't know what your business is,' Fess told him, but Wade's tone had hinted at a little hostility towards him. Right at that moment Fess wished he'd been able to get a message to Charlie before leaving Pottersville, had been able to point him towards Hot Springs in case these two men were more suspicious of his story than they had so far pretended to be.

Again, Fess's right hand moved minutely closer to his gun. In the darkness he sensed, rather than saw, that Tom's horse had drawn closer, and although Wade was the one doing the talking he knew that they were working in unison. Even so, when Tom snatched the pistol from Fess's holster, he was surprised both by the act and the fact that Tom was so near.

'Hey!' Fess shouted. 'What's the idea?'

'Easy,' said Wade, 'have a slug of water. Wash some of that dust you don't like from your throat.'

'Give me my gun,' said Fess.

'You're among friends. You don't need a gun.'

'You've got yours.' Fess turned in the saddle to look at Tom who was holding the captured weapon with intent.

Wade spoke again, disregarding Fess Salter's comment completely. 'Tell us again about your meeting with Clint Revlon.'

'What's to tell? I met him in Pine Bluff. He told me to seek him out in Pottersville if I needed work. Didn't mention Hot Springs.'

'And the work he promised, what did that entail?'

'He wasn't specific.' While he talked Fess fidgeted in the saddle, turning right and left as though trying to include both men in the conversation as he gave his answers. In fact it was a ruse to cover the little movements of his horse, causing it to turn so that both his adversaries were only able to see its left flank. He didn't know why Wade and Tom had chosen this moment to disarm him, whether he'd made an error and given them just cause to suspect him or if they had always intended to question him further once clear of town, but he knew that his story was flimsy and once broken they would kill him. He was no good to anyone dead. Although his rifle was still in its scabbard under his right leg he knew that he had no hope of drawing and firing it before Tom pulled the trigger of the pistol. What he was able to do, however, was surreptitiously unhitch the coil of rope hanging from the saddle horn.

'Didn't mention raids against the Union invaders?'

'No,' said Fess, the loops of rope clutched firmly in his right hand. He jiggled again so that the horse moved its back quarters giving him a better angle from which to strike.

Wade, who hadn't drawn his own gun, chose that moment to step out of the saddle which gave Fess a better opportunity to attack than he might have expected. Swinging the bunched rope in a short arc he slapped the pistol out of Tom's hand and pulled at the reins to turn his horse's head in a dash for freedom. In the darkness and confined space in which they'd halted, flight was not easily executed. Fess rode his horse straight into the flank of

Wade's mount and it almost went down.

Behind him, Tom was cursing and Fess figured he was trying to draw his own gun to put an end to his resistance, but it was Wade who acted most decisively. Although dismounted, he still held the reins of his horse and when, in the midst of the mêlée, it was struck by Fess Salter's horse, the startled beast almost pulled Wade off his feet. However, like Fess, Wade was an old soldier with well-honed survival instincts. He released the hold he had on the horse and reached for Fess, grabbing a handful of his shirt. The combination of stumbling horse and hauling man were enough to drag Fess from his beast's back but not without a fight. He regained the presence of mind to throw a kick at Wade and was rewarded with a satisfying thud and yell as he connected. Fess suspected that the rowel of his spur had cut the man's face but he couldn't be certain. He hit the ground hard but was quickly on his feet and making his way down the short incline to the trail below.

Wade's voice was a mix of pain and anger when he yelled his orders to Tom. 'Get him.'

Tom, his fist now filled with his revolver, fired into the night.

'Don't shoot yet, fool,' yelled Wade. 'You might hit me or one of the horses. Catch him in the open.'

Fess had momentarily been swallowed by the darkness but Tom spurred his horse in pursuit. Wade grasped at the rifle in his saddle-boot and followed in their wake.

The ground was uneven and littered with rocks and stones of various sizes. Fess stumbled, the noise carrying to his pursuers informing them of the direction he'd taken. He knew that his life was now forfeit and the moment either one of them got a clear shot at him he would be a dead man. He crouched as he ran and pulled from his boot a long, thin-bladed knife that he always carried. He could inflict injuries on his enemies with the weapon, but only if he got close enough to use it.

Fess stumbled and fell and tumbled downhill uttering oaths at his clumsiness. A shot was fired, then another; both slugs struck the ground some yards behind. The darkness of the night was still Fess Salter's best ally but he knew now, a-foot, he had little hope of escape. He could hear Tom urging his mount down the short incline in pursuit and knew that he was more interested in killing than asking questions. Fess scrambled to his feet and plunged on into the night, hoping to find a refuge that would provide a more solid barricade from bullets than that provided by the lack of light.

Wade's voice barked above the dull sound of hoofs drumming against the ground. 'Can you see him?'

'Yeah. He's reached the road.' Tom fired two more shots, either to prove to Wade that he was in command of the situation and their quarry was close to capture or to prove to Fess that he couldn't escape. The truth of the matter was that those bullets were no threat, flying several yards away from Fess. At the same moment, a collection of boulders appeared to his left and he dashed towards them.

The two largest boulders were chest high but Fess would have to lie down to get any sort of protection from the rest of the collection. That wasn't an option, once he was on the ground he would be at their mercy. Nonetheless, his immediate need forced him to seek the sanctuary that the two larger boulders could provide and he reached them just as a bullet struck the nearest rock and ricocheted across the empty terrain.

As Fess crouched behind the biggest rock he heard Tom's call of triumph. 'He's cornered, Wade.' The sound of the horse slowing to walking pace reached Fess. He gripped the knife, his mind working out a plan as his enemy came closer. If he could lure him within striking distance he could kill him then flee from Wade on Tom's horse. Fess remained crouched, listening to the steady clip-clop of the approaching horse. It was walking, an indication that Tom had no fear of Fess, that an unarmed man couldn't harm him. The beast was close now, coming around the right-hand side of the boulders.

Fess prepared to attack. He would have only one opportunity. If he didn't strike first and with lethal accuracy, he would most probably be killed. But if he could win the horse he might yet escape the fate that Wade and Tom planned for him. He pressed closer against the rock, tried to get deeper into the darkness in order to use the element of surprise to its full effect. The horse's head appeared and Fess's leg muscles tightened in preparation to spring forward. Then the rest of the horse appeared and Fess stepped forward but made no other move. There was no one in the saddle.

'Looking for me?' asked a voice behind him.

Fess turned slowly. Tom had circled

around the other side of the boulders and now stood with a taunting grin on his face, his legs slightly apart and his pistol pointed at Fess Salter's stomach.

'Reckon you are a blue-belly spy,' said Tom, and he pulled the trigger.

A metallic click sounded as the hammer fell on an empty chamber. In the silent night it was a noise almost as loud as the expected explosion of gunpowder and it had the same effect. A man died. Fess reacted first to the unexpected turn of events, stepping forward and thrusting his knife deep into Tom's chest. He twisted the blade, withdrew it and plunged it in again. With his face twisted grotesquely by the fiery pain, Tom fell to the ground and with a final gurgle of sound, died.

'Tom!' called a voice some yards back along the trail.

Tom's horse, Fess Salter's means of escape, had wandered away, perhaps startled by the moment of violence and smell of blood. Fess prepared to follow it but out of the corner of his eye he caught sight of the figure that was closing on him.

Wade, at first bustling forward in the certainty that his partner would have recaptured the unarmed Fess, had halted to take in the scene before him. The sight of Fess with a blood-covered knife in his hand standing over Tom's body evoked a grunt of anger. 'Boss wanted to be sure you were lying about Clint Revlon,' he snarled, 'and I guess this proves it.' He raised the rifle he carried to his shoulder and prepared to fire.

This time, Fess considered the situation hopeless. He still held the knife that had helped him to overcome Tom but now it was useless. It wasn't even possible to throw the knife before Wade pulled the trigger. Fess faced his adversary and waited for the bullet that would surely end his life.

However, it was another gun that fired first. The shot, which came from behind Wade, spun him round so that he crumpled to the ground with his legs twisted and his face looking up at the sky.

'That was close,' said Charlie Jefferson, 'it took longer than I expected to catch up.'

# 7

It took only a few moments for Charlie to relate his recognition of Wade in the livery stable and the handful of words that had convinced him that Fess was in danger. 'So I followed,' he said, 'but you were farther ahead than I figured.'

'I'm not complaining,' Fess told him.

'The question is, what do we do now?'

'Head for Hot Springs,' Fess said. 'We know Clint Revlon is there and is connected with the bunch of riders we're hunting.'

Charlie wasn't convinced that that was a good idea. 'This is an organized bunch we're dealing with,' he told Fess, 'the two we killed will be expected either to arrive in Hot Springs with you or back at Pottersville without you. When they don't, someone will want to know what happened to them and they'll be looking for you to supply the answer. You won't be safe in either place and you need to keep away from Clint Revlon.'

'He's our best chance of locating the gang,' Fess mused.

Charlie wasn't forgetting that the boss was back in Pottersville but they didn't know his identity, so he had to agree with Fess that the fiery Clint was the best option. 'The night hostler at the Pottersville livery could lead us to the boss,' he said, 'but I've already been in that town twice and another sudden visit might seem suspicious. I reckon in the morning I'll tie these two across their saddles and take them on to Hot Springs. Perhaps they'll arouse some interest and lead me to more gang members.'

'What about me?' asked Fess.

'Find a place to camp outside town. I'll find you when I need you.'

So that was the plan they put into action. After Fess had helped to hoist the bodies on to the horses he rode ahead and found a location in the high ground which overlooked the trail into Hot Springs. Charlie waited until the sun had climbed above that high ground before setting off for town. He didn't want to get there before people were going about their business. As it was, he barely encountered anyone along the trail, only two teamsters with long wagons who watched his approach, studied the bundles slung across the saddles of the trailing horses but offered no comment and asked no questions. That was the war, Charlie figured, it had taught men not to interfere in events that were not relevant to their own business.

When he reached town it was a different matter. The first people who saw him watched in silence as he passed, but the deeper he rode into Hot Springs the larger the group of people who followed him became.

'Where's the sheriff's office?' Charlie asked.

'You're heading in the right direction,' the nearest fellow told him. 'Who have you got there?'

'I don't know. Found the pair five miles back.'

'Hey,' somebody further back among the crowd shouted, 'this is Tom Galbraith.' Charlie looked back to see that the speaker had lifted the head of the man slung across the last horse.

Amid a host of exclamations of surprise, one voice rose above the others. 'Somebody run and get his pa, quickly.'

By the time Charlie reached the office of the law the other body had been identified as Wade Mason but his death didn't excite the crowd in the same manner. The sheriff and a deputy came out on to the boardwalk as Charlie stepped down from the saddle. The deputy lifted the heads of the dead men and confirmed the identities.

'Who are you and what happened?' The sheriff's tone was accusatory.

'The name's Charlie Jefferson and I

don't know what happened. Found these bodies back along the trail and I wasn't carrying a shovel to bury them.'

'What made you think they belonged here?'

'Nothing. I was heading this way so I brought them with me. Would you prefer I'd just left them to rot?'

'I'm not sure I like your attitude,' said the sheriff.

It was only to be expected that bringing in the bodies of townsmen would arouse some suspicion that he was their slayer, but the sheriff seemed openly hostile which could make it difficult for Charlie to make any progress in Hot Springs. He wanted to announce his true feelings, that enough good men had rotted where they fell over the last four years, but casting himself as a pacifist wasn't likely to draw other Red Mask members to him. 'What you like, sheriff, goes hand-in-hand with those two dead men, not my concern.'

'Here comes Henry,' the deputy said.

Everyone turned to see a tall man with greying hair, rimless specs and a long white apron hurrying along the street. The crowd parted to let the man through to the horses that still bore the bodies. He glanced at the sheriff with the hope in his eyes that he'd been misinformed by the message he'd received. The sheriff's unflinching stance shattered that hope. He rested his big hand on the body of his son. 'How did it happen?' he asked.

'Jayhawkers, Henry. I reckon they ambushed your boy and Wade. This fellow found them this morning.'

Charlie looked quizzically at the sheriff, unsure what knowledge he possessed to reach such a conclusion, but he said nothing to contradict the lawman. Henry Galbraith, he figured, would need a few minutes to mourn his son before demanding details. It was then that Charlie realized that Henry Galbraith was not alone. A slim figure had followed him through the crowd. Her hair was dark, tied back with a dull red ribbon and she wore a simple grey dress which didn't flatter her in any way. Tears were running down her face but seemed to be doing so at their own behest because her face was composed. Henry put an arm around her shoulder, intending to turn her away from the bodies on the horses, but she was determined and needed to confirm the identity of at least one of the dead men for herself. Even then she maintained a stoic expression as she turned her gaze towards Charlie. She wiped a hand across her face and seemed surprised to find that it was wet, but this distracted her for less than a moment.

'Jayhawkers,' she called to Charlie, her voice steady, 'perhaps you are one of them.'

Henry Galbraith caught her arm and tried to prevent any confrontation. 'Your brother is dead, Harriet, this isn't the time,' he said.

Charlie Jefferson was confused by his thoughts. He wasn't a jayhawker, one of those ex-Union soldiers who, like bushwhackers, were prepared to use violence to take from the people of the southern states whatever they wanted, but he was riding for the army and the die-hard believers of the confederacy saw little difference between jayhawkers and uniformed soldiers. Hot Springs, it seemed to Charlie, was reluctant to let go of its confederacy support which meant that he was probably in the right place to find other members of the Red Masks gang but that his life would be forfeit if his identity was discovered. That was the risk he'd accepted when he'd ridden into town and the knowledge that Tom Galbraith had intended to kill Fess Salter in cold blood enabled him to temper any compassion he felt for the girl's grief.

'Miss,' he called, his voice retaining the hard edge that had been in evidence when talking to the sheriff, 'I'm a stranger to this area so I don't suppose there's any good reason why you should believe me, but all I know about jayhawkers is what I've read in newspapers. I'm sorry your brother is dead but he didn't go down without a fight, his gun was empty when I picked it up.'

Charlie wasn't sure why he'd added the last sentence. It could have been to prove that Tom Galbraith had not been an innocent victim of the violence, or perhaps it had been to give the girl some comfort in the knowledge that her brother had stood his ground and fought to the last.

The girl didn't respond. Her father, leading the horse that carried his son's body, guided her away from the throng. Someone took the lead rein of the other horse and followed behind, heading for the undertaker's parlour which was some distance down the street.

The sheriff ushered Charlie into his office, recorded the details of his find then questioned him about his plans. 'Just riding through?'

'I thought I might hang around for a couple of days. I'm looking for work. Anyone hiring around here?'

'Ex-soldier?'

That's right. Does it make a difference?'

'Could be.'

'The war is over, isn't it?'

'According to Washington. As you found out for yourself, people are still being killed around here.'

'Any particular reason for blaming jayhawkers?'

'Who else would it be?'

'Back in Pottersville it was bush-whackers who were being accused of crimes.'

'Different circumstances there,' said the sheriff. 'The carpetbaggers moved in without much opposition so the bushwhackers are striking at the Union lovers. Here, no one wants the northern influence. Henry Galbraith has turned down two offers for his business so I guess the frustrated carpetbaggers summoned up the jayhawkers to prove they won't be resisted forever.'

Charlie quit the sheriff's office with the belief that a true peace would be a long time coming. The northern speculators were determined to subjugate and impoverish the people of the south using whatever means necessary, and remnants of the vanquished army were prepared to shed every drop of blood to thwart them. Charlie wanted an end to the fighting but now knew that the task was bigger than defeating isolated bands of bushwhackers.

The Grand Hotel was across the street and two blocks down from the sheriff's office. It was mainly stone-built, three storeys high and Charlie was given a room that overlooked the main street. Having found accommodation for himself he then stabled his horse, handing over a dollar to cover feed and shelter for two nights. It was well past midday when he picked out a restaurant that had venison stew on the menu and more than one vacant table. He picked up the sense that he was recognized by more than one customer but no one spoke to him and he sat beside a window which gave him a commanding view of the street.

That was when Charlie saw Clint Revlon, although it was another man who first caught his attention. That man's gait was awkward, an old injury which forced him to favour his left leg. He was a stocky, rough-looking man in need of a shave and the trail dust beaten out of his clothes. Charlie's interest in him wouldn't have lasted more than a moment if it hadn't been for the furtive manner in which he paused on the boardwalk and studied the street before going into the telegraph office. When he emerged he sat on a bench outside the office and there, a few minutes later, almost coinciding with the arrival of Charlie's stew, he was joined by Clint Revlon.

Charlie watched the duo while he dined. Revlon appeared agitated but his constant pacing was in keeping with the other occasions that Charlie had seen him. The other fellow was less animated but nothing in their discussion was giving him pleasure. Fifteen minutes later the telegraph clerk stepped outside and gave the man a message which he and Clint Revlon studied together. Charlie had no doubt that it had been instigated by the deaths of Tom Galbraith and Wade Mason. By the time he'd finished his meal the others had quit their position outside the telegraph office and were nowhere to be seen.

For the remainder of the day, Charlie hung around town with no plan in mind other than to let anyone interested in him know that he had no intention of quitting the place before morning. He sat awhile on the hotel porch, on the bench outside the telegraph office and on the boardwalk outside The Cotton Queen, which was the busiest saloon in town. He exchanged 'Good day,' with some of the townsmen but no one made any attempt to extend the greeting into any form of conversation although he was sure that some of them recognized him as the man who had brought the bodies to town. Even the sheriff, who had watched Charlie's perambulation from his office window, merely touched his hat in greeting when his evening patrol took him past the spot where Charlie sat.

The interior of The Cotton Queen consisted of two tight rooms where the men of Hot Springs gathered to air grievances and pleasures in the habit of men around the world. Each room had a long counter where customers stood in groups or leaned in solitude, participating in or listening to alcohol fuelled conversations. That day, the death of Tom Galbraith was the subject of several conversations and Charlie, having stepped inside when darkness fell, learned that the Galbraith family was long established in this territory. Curiously, although there were mutterings of sympathy for the family's loss, few were expressed for Tom. There were shrugs and head shakes when his name was mentioned as though a violent death came as no surprise. Wade

Mason, it transpired, was not a citizen of Hot Springs. In fact no one was certain where he hailed from but he had turned up infrequently during the weeks since the end of the war.

Charlie listened to the snippets of conversation that were taking place around him but couldn't identify anyone who might have had a friendship with either Tom or Wade. The only information he learned that might prove useful to him was that the funeral of both men was due to take place the next day. He promised himself to be there. Clint Revlon would surely be there which would give Charlie an opportunity to make contact with him.

There were few people abroad when Charlie headed back to the Grand Hotel that night. He wondered how Fess was faring in the high ground outside town and how long his patience would keep him there. However, Charlie wasn't too concerned. Unlike himself, always eager for action, the older man had been relaxed during periods of inactivity during the war, and had shown little anxiety when a battle was looming.

Charlie considered his current situation, keen to get to grips with the Red Masks and earn the reward of which Fess had spoken, wanting to fill his saddlebags so that he could return home with the fortune he'd promised Ruth Prescott. At that moment, blonde-haired Ruth filled his mind as she had done on so many nights during the fighting.

'Hey!' the call came from behind Charlie, disrupting his thoughts.

He turned but no one was there. Then suddenly he was smothered by a blanket that was thrown over his head and strong arms gripped him from behind. He could hear footsteps, there was more than one person, and despite his struggles he was being dragged backwards away from the main street.

Without warning, someone drove their fist into Charlie's stomach and the air left his body with a pain-filled grunt. Someone, perhaps the same person although Charlie believed that more than two people were attacking him, grabbed his lower legs and he was quickly carried for several yards. As soon as Charlie had refilled his lungs he tried to kick out but achieved neither freedom nor damage to his assailants.

A muffled voice spoke. 'Don't hit him again. We need him to talk.' No sooner were those words uttered than his feet were dropped to the ground and he was pushed hard in the chest so that he stumbled backwards into a wall. The blanket was pulled from his head and he found himself confronted by a semi-circle of five men. They all wore hoods over their heads. Red Masks. Charlie rubbed at his stomach as though still suffering the effects of the blow.

For a moment there was silence then the man in the middle of the group spoke. 'Who are you?'

'What business is it of yours?'

'We'll ask the questions. What's your name?'

Charlie had achieved his first goal, he'd met up with the gang he was hunting. Now he had to gain some credence with them, identify them and hope to find a way to get them into the hands of the military. He glowered, showed his anger at the unjustified abduction and tightened his lips, an indication of obstinacy and unwillingness to talk.

At a signal from the man who'd spoken, two men stepped forward, one at each side, and they grabbed Charlie's arms. Before Charlie could resist, a third man punched him twice in the stomach and would have done so again if the speaker hadn't forbidden it. With light steps the hitter moved back, his eagerness to deliver more punishment was apparent in the way his hands still formed fists and were held in readiness, chest high. Charlie had grunted as the blows landed but he'd been prepared and had ridden them the best he was able, to lessen their effect.

'Your name?'

Charlie shook his head until the hitter's shoulders jumped in that way that predicted he was coming forward to strike again. 'Charlie Jefferson. I've got no money. I'm looking for work.'

'Where's your partner?'

'Partner? I don't know who you mean.'

'The guy who left Pottersville before you with Tom and Wade, the one who helped you kill them.'

'You're talking nonsense,' said Charlie. 'I didn't kill those men. I found their bodies and brought them back to town. Why would I bring them to town if I killed them?'

'A good question, but you don't deny being in Pottersville, do you?'

'Sure I was in Pottersville. It's not a secret.'

The fifth man, the man who had so far taken no part in the confrontation, spoke next. 'Why did you return to Pottersville? You left in the morning, returned before nightfall then lit out for Hot Springs when it grew dark. What was that all about?'

Charlie was surprised that his movements had been monitored but he thought he saw an opportunity to turn it to his advantage. 'I'm looking for work,' he said. 'I'd heard there were opportunities down south in the timberland but down by the Ouachita there'd been another killing. Two men. An army unit almost caught me with them. I didn't want to hang around with soldiers in the vicinity but I couldn't cross the river without them seeing me so I returned to Pottersville. I'd intended to stay there overnight and try to make it south the next day but I heard someone talking about rounding up stray cattle in Texas to sell to work camps. I thought I'd give it a try. I'm heading for Texas.'

The first interrogator spoke again. 'You've got reason to run from the army?'

'No more than most,' replied Charlie

but he put such a tone to his voice that the opposite was implied. 'I know the war is over but it's hard to break some habits.'

'Haven't you got a home to go to?'

'It'll take a good deal more money than I currently have to put the place right. That's why I'm looking for work.'

The five men exchanged glances. Four of them looked ready to end the confrontation, only the hitter disagreed. 'You can't let him go,' he declared, the agitated movements increased, stepping close to Charlie, staring into his eyes, his hand straying to the gun at his side.

Charlie saw the movement and his gaze followed the hitter's hand. He looked at the gunbelt around the man's waist and even in the darkness he could see the newness of the leather holster, recognized the intricate filigree with which Dave Willis had been so pleased.

The hitter drew his gun. 'We've got to kill him,' he said.

'I'll make the decisions,' said the fifth man, who stepped forward and drew his own gun. 'Can't have you following us,' he told Charlie and with a sudden, violent swing, smashed the barrel of his revolver across Charlie's head.

# 8

Charlie had just finished swilling cold water from the jug on the dresser over his head when the knock sounded sharp and sudden on his door. It was the sheriff.

'Heard you'd run into some trouble,' he said, casting his eyes over the discoloured swelling at the side of Charlie's head.

'News travels fast considering I haven't spoken to anyone.'

'The night clerk downstairs saw you come in. His message interrupted my breakfast but I thought I'd better come and get some details.'

'Nothing to tell you, sheriff. Some men thought I might have killed the two I brought in yesterday but it seems I convinced them I didn't do it.'

The sheriff pointed at the lump.

'That's evidence that they think you are innocent?'

'If they'd thought otherwise my body would have been found in the alley where they questioned me.'

'Can you identify the men?'

The fancy gun holster that had belonged to Dave Willis flashed through Charlie's mind. 'No. They all wore hoods.' If he had any hope of getting closer to the gang it wouldn't be done by spilling what he knew to the law.

'Red hoods?' asked the sheriff.

'Could have been but it was too dark to be certain. Is it significant?'

The sheriff's expression was sceptical, even a stranger had surely heard of the renegade bands in the area. 'They could have been Red Masks,' he said.

'The bushwhackers who attacked Pine Bluff? Their name was on everyone's lips in Pottersville.' He paused. 'Why would the Red Masks care about the killings?'

The sheriff pulled at his gunbelt, lifted it higher on his hips, not with any intention of using his guns, more a habit when he needed time to think.

'Rumours,' he said at last.

'Rumours!' repeated Charlie and waited for an explanation.

'Tom Galbraith wasn't a man to keep his opinions to himself. His thoughts about Lee's surrender, carpetbaggers and southerners who've embraced the peace were voiced often enough.'

'You think he was a Red Mask?'

'I have no evidence to support that,' the sheriff told Charlie, 'but his sympathies were with them, as are those of a lot of people in this town.'

If Tom Galbraith had been involved with the Red Masks — and Charlie had every reason to suppose he had — then the likelihood that others would turn up at the funeral seemed more than probable. Apart from his recognition of Dave Willis's gunbelt, Charlie also kept to himself the knowledge that one of his attackers had ridden through from Pottersville to identify him. What the sheriff had said about the prejudice of the townspeople made Charlie cautious about divulging information and surprised, too, that he was unable to exclude the sheriff from a bias in favour of the Red Masks.

The one piece of information that was abundantly clear was that the bushwhackers were on the lookout for Fess Salter which meant that he wasn't safe, either in Hot Springs or Pottersville. When a suitable opportunity arose, Charlie would have to seek out and warn his friend.

A copy of the *Hot Springs Advertiser*, which he read over breakfast in the hotel, gave him an idea for getting out of town without too many questions being asked. In fact, by asking directions of the hotel clerk, he was quite sure that his reason for leaving town would be spread quickly enough. A couple of articles had caught his eye, both of which concerned a boom in business. One story featured a sawmill at a place called Cherokee Creek, and the other

136

was about a wagon-maker at Forster's Bend.

'If these fellows are doing so well,' Charlie told the hotel clerk, 'perhaps they need an extra pair of hands.'

'Do you intend to settle in our town?' asked the clerk.

'Just long enough to earn a grubstake that'll take me back west. There are pockets of land in the Wyoming Territory that are ideal for farming, but first I need money for equipment, seed and livestock. The faster I get it the quicker I'll move on.'

'Wyoming Territory, is that your home?'

Charlie continued to spin his story, embellishing the truth to make it palatable for southern sympathizers. 'That's where my family now live. They were Virginians originally. I came back to fight when the war began.' It was clear that the clerk was a natural tittle-tattle. His eyes almost sparkled as he absorbed all the snippets he was being fed and Charlie had no doubt that he would be just as happy relating them later to anyone who would listen. Charlie didn't find this sinister, he'd often observed that all hotel clerks were gossips.

'I almost ended my days in Virginia,' he told the man. He patted his left shoulder. 'Hit by shrapnel at Sayler's Creek.' He didn't tell the clerk he'd sustained the wound fighting with the Union army, allowed him to assume he'd been with the Confederates.

Armed with directions to Cherokee Creek and Forster's Bend, Charlie got his horse from the livery stable and rode out of town. He rode south-westerly, his plan being to establish his story by first visiting the sawmill at Cherokee Creek then following the river north to Forster's Bend. He would complete the circle back to Hot Springs by passing through the high country where Fess was camped. They would meet as he returned to town which would give Charlie plenty of opportunity to spot anyone on his trail. His interrogation by the Red Masks had made it clear that he'd been under scrutiny in Pottersville when he was an innocent traveller, so in Hot Springs, where people openly suspected him of involvement in the deaths of Tom Galbraith and Wade Mason, it seemed probable that he was being watched more closely.

Although the sawmill owners weren't looking for extra workmen, Frank Jameson, the wagon builder, confessed that an extra pair of hands about the place would be useful. However, brisk as business was at the present time, he couldn't offer Charlie better than a billet, meals and a couple of dollars a week until he was sure that the boom would last. 'Way things are going around here,' Frank declared, 'the government won't be happy until all southern businesses have been swept away to make profit for the northerners.'

Charlie had ridden on, heading for the high country, completing his sweep back to Hot Springs. He hadn't pushed the pace above a canter for the whole journey and he'd taken several opportunities to halt, pretending to study the land but in fact checking his back-trail for followers. Only once, between Comanche Creek and Forster's Bend, did he detect movement among the trees. He watched for several minutes but the movement was not repeated. Eventually he attributed it to some wild, hunting beast.

Three miles from Hot Springs, picking his way down a stony incline to intersect the trail, Fess emerged from between two high boulders to block his path.

'I was getting lonely,' he grumbled, 'and anxious to know what was happening in Hot Springs. I was figuring on riding in when it got dark.'

'You can't do that,' Charlie told him. They dismounted and led their horses up amongst the boulders where they wouldn't be seen by anyone passing on the trail below.

Charlie told Fess everything that had happened since they'd parted.

'You seem troubled, Charlie,' Fess said after listening to his friend.

'What I don't like,' Charlie replied, 'is that the army seems to be concentrating on the ex-Confederate bands when the jayhawkers are causing as much trouble.'

'I reckon that's because the bushwhackers think they are still trying to fight a war. The government can't let them continue.'

'But the people, Fess, those who are suffering because they won't submit to the demands of the carpetbaggers, are also due protection.'

'The way I understand it, Charlie, the carpetbaggers aren't breaking any laws, and if someone thinks they are then they get the local lawman to deal with it. Bushwhackers are a federal cause, that's why the army is involved, and we're employed by the army. We can't fight everyone, Charlie. We've got to take one step at a time. Let's finish off this Red Mask gang before tackling the next evil.'

'Finish off the Red Masks,' snarled a voice behind them. It was the man with the limp, the man who had sent and received telegraph messages the previous day. He held a revolver in his hand, covering Charlie and Fess with it while beckoning someone forward with his left hand. 'I knew that you were a Union spy,' he told Charlie.

Charlie didn't recognize the second man but he was of a height and build that matched a couple of the men who had attacked him in Hot Springs. At that moment, though, it was irrelevant. This man, too, carried a pistol and his cold eyes warned that he was prepared to use it.

Fess uttered a low grunt, a sign that he was disappointed that he had relaxed his vigilance sufficient to allow these men to get so close. Ten yards separated the newcomers from the spot where he and Charlie sat, which was a distance he couldn't allow to diminish. He'd swiftly assessed the two who confronted them as men accustomed to gunplay but he knew that an element of luck was associated with hitting a target with a handgun at such a distance. If the men had been armed with rifles there would have been no luck involved. Even so, if he and Charlie made a move for their own guns there was a major risk of being wounded and incapacitated, but it was a risk they must take. From the moment the man's voice had carried across the space between them, Fess had not looked at Charlie. He hoped that his friend's thoughts were running in conjunction with his own, that when he moved Charlie would move too. Out of the corner of his eye he could see the slight movement of Charlie's legs, his muscles tightening as he prepared to launch himself away from the place where he sat.

The limper was speaking again, his words this time aimed at Fess. 'You must be the fellow who spun the yarn about meeting Clint Revlon in Pine

Bluff, the one who left Pottersville with Tom and Wade. You get around.'

'Sure do,' Fess agreed, 'but I don't stay in one place long.' As if those words were a rehearsed signal, both Fess and Charlie threw themselves away from the boulders on which they were sitting. Fess dived to his left, seeking the shelter of a cluster of small boulders, and drew his pistol as he hit the ground. He fired a shot in the direction of his enemies and heard it sing away into the empty landscape as it glanced off a high rock.

Meanwhile, Charlie had tumbled backwards, finding sanctuary behind the boulder on which he'd been sitting. A bullet struck the rock, bounced and took a snippet from the brim of his hat. Instantly, his gun was in his hand. Raising his head sufficiently, he was able to see the two bushwhackers heading for rock protection of their own. Charlie drew a bead on the limper and fired. The man staggered, the gun fell from his hand and his arm stretched out as though hoping his comrade would grab it and pull him to safety. But there was no rescue for him. He sank to his knees, his mouth gaped as though wanting to express some profound knowledge but no words were uttered. Taking the opportunity to aim carefully, Charlie's second shot struck the limper in the chest. He collapsed, full-length on the ground, never to move again.

The second man, seeing the demise of his companion, made a dash for the boulders around which he and the limper had first appeared. Fess fired, but the distance had widened and his bullet whistled over the man's shoulder. Then he was out of sight of Fess and Charlie. They rose to their feet.

'He's going for his horse,' shouted Fess.

'We can't let him reach town,' Charlie replied, knowing that any hope of infiltrating the gang would be lost if the man was able to report what he knew to anyone else.

Fess, although older, reacted more quickly and with agility. The fitness acquired during his long years living in the Rockies had not forsaken him. Even so, by the time he'd reached the boulders the sound of hoofbeats could be heard. The man was urging his mount down the slope towards the trail and for a second Fess considered firing a shot at him but he knew it would be nothing but a futile gesture. He needed a rifle but his own was twenty-five yards back with his horse.

As though their thoughts were the output of one mind, Charlie, when he reached Fess Salter's side, said, 'There's a rifle on the other horse.'

Sure enough, the stock of a Springfield rifle protruded from the saddle boot of the limper's horse. Dashing forward, Fess grabbed the rifle and tried to get the bushwhacker in his sights but by this time he was almost at the trail and turning towards Hot Springs.

Charlie cursed. 'Lost him,' he said.

'Not yet,' grunted Fess who departed at a fast, stooped lope. Keeping to the high ground he leapt from boulder to boulder with barely a break in stride. During his sojourn in this high ground he'd had the opportunity to study the terrain and knew that the trail to Hot Springs followed the contours of the land and, at this point, looped half-way around the hillside. If he was quick enough, if he could reach the other side of the hill in less time than a galloping horse could cover a mile, he could prevent the Red Mask rider reaching Hot Springs.

It was touch and go. Fess heard the thundering hoof beats as he reached the summit that overlooked the trail on the other side of the hill. Although he knew that his first priority was to stop the man reaching Hot Springs, Fess had a hankering to capture him alive and get him back to Colonel Crook at Fort Smith. Under proper interrogation he was likely to give up the names of the other gang members. But taking the man prisoner would not be easily achieved. He would get only one chance to succeed and if he failed then he and Charlie would have to quit the area with their mission a failure.

Halfway down the hillside, a large flat rock gave him a commanding view of the trail below. He paused, knowing that if he waited here, prone on the ground with the rifle tight against his shoulder — a position he'd adopted many times during the war — he could kill the bushwhacker with one shot. It was the sensible thing to do, the certain way to prevent the man from disclosing Charlie's role as an agent for the army, but the war was over and killing from ambush no longer sat easy with him. He moved on, sometimes running, sometimes jumping and sometimes sliding, hoping that he wasn't raising either too much dust or too much noise to betray his position. Fess kept going, fixing his course on a bluff which overhung the trail, a point which he was sure he could reach before his enemy.

The approaching horseman cast glances behind, as though fearful that he was being pursued. At this point the trail sloped uphill and the horse, which had been asked to run at its full extent over difficult terrain, now needed a breather. Its pace dropped as it passed under the bluff which overhung the trail and its rider threw one more look over his shoulder.

Dropping the rifle as he stepped forward, Fess launched himself on to the back of the bushwhacker. The combination of Fess's weight and the surprise attack were sufficient to drag the man from his saddle. Together they rolled on the hard, dusty trail, both grunting with the impact and thrusting arms and legs at the other in the hope of gaining the upper hand. Eventually it was the bushwhacker who achieved the most leverage with his legs and thrust them apart, his momentum was halted but Fess rolled on a few yards down the slope at the other side of the trail.

'There's no escape,' yelled Fess as he

struggled to his knees. 'I'm taking you back to Fort Smith to answer for your crimes.'

The bushwhacker, however, was barely listening to Fess. His hand was busy, drawing his revolver from its holster and raising with deliberate aim. Fess threw himself to the side, pulling his own gun free. Any hopes of taking the man alive disappeared at that moment. Hurriedly, the rebel fired his first shot. The bullet struck the ground some distance behind Fess. The bushwhacker's second shot had greater accuracy. The bullet tugged at the shoulder of Fess Salter's jacket but failed to inflict any injury. It proved to be his last shot because almost simultaneously, Fess discharged his own weapon. That bullet struck his opponent in the stomach and, as the surprised bushwhacker grabbed at the wound, Fess fired again, his aim a little higher, the lump of lead smacking into his chest, throwing him to the ground, dead.

It was with a sigh of relief that Fess saw the bushwhacker's horse had not careered on its way into town but was standing a few yards away. After dragging the body off the road and hiding it among the rocks he caught the horse and rode back to the place where he'd left Charlie.

Charlie greeted him waving a red hood. 'I found this in the saddle-bag,' he said, and an inspection of the saddle-bags on the horse that Fess was riding produced another hood.

'These dispel any dispute that they were Red Mask riders,' said Fess. 'Perhaps they'll come in useful.'

'I've got a problem,' Charlie said. 'If those men were acting on orders then someone's going to wonder why I've returned to Hot Springs and they haven't.'

After a while they agreed on a course of action. It was unlikely to clear Charlie of total suspicion but it would, at least, give him some sort of alibi. He rode on towards town leaving Fess to execute the plan.

# 9

Charlie Jefferson established his presence in Hot Springs more than an hour before the funeral procession moved slowly along Main Street to the white-walled church and its graveyard beyond. Returning to town, he'd sat awhile on the porch outside the Grand Hotel then, as though uncomfortable in the late-afternoon heat, swiped beads of sweat from his brow as he sauntered down to The Cotton Queen for a cold beer. There, in keeping with what he'd told the hotel clerk earlier, he told the barman he was looking for work but had been unable to find any either at the sawmill or with the wagon builder at Forster's Bend. He'd kept his voice low, as though the beer server was a confidant to whom he was imparting a personal grumble. Charlie knew it wasn't necessary to draw attention by being loud and brash; being a stranger, any utterance in a town like Hot Springs would spread quickly enough. It was enough, at this time, to be noted around town by independent witnesses and have them repeat his need for money. The way he continually hitched the gunbelt around his waist conveyed the impression that he wouldn't be too fussy about how he got it.

After leaving The Cotton Queen, he sat for a while outside the telegraph office then moved along the street and was leaning against a post that supported an upper balcony outside the newspaper office when the funeral procession came into view. Four black horses adorned with black plumes pulled an open wagon on which two coffins lay side-by-side. Behind this, in Indian file, came three buggies which had been washed and polished for the occasion. The first carried the Galbraith family. Henry was driving and Charlie assumed that the dumpy woman at his side was his wife. Harriet Galbraith, her face covered by a black veil, was on the seat behind. She turned her head in Charlie's direction as they passed but nothing in her expression indicated that she recognized him.

Charlie didn't know the occupants of the other buggies and barely recognized any of the hundred or so people who walked in their wake, but Clint Revlon was there, one of a bunch of men at the back of the cortege. One of the men passed a comment and half-a-dozen pairs of eyes swung in Charlie's direction. Charlie pretended not to notice but he was sure that Clint and the others were surprised that he was in town. More comments were exchanged among the group and heads shaken in denial. Charlie could only assume that it was the absence of the limper and his friend that was under discussion. He was still watching the trail of mourners when a voice interrupted his thoughts.

'I'll walk along with you.' The sheriff was at Charlie's side and indicating that he should join those heading for the graveyard.

'Funerals are family affairs,' Charlie said, 'I didn't know the men.'

'You mean to hang around Hot Springs, don't you? Then a gesture of respect won't go amiss.' The sheriff stepped off the boardwalk still talking, giving Charlie no alternative but to fall in step with him. 'Heard you rode out this morning looking for work.'

'Without success,' Charlie told him.

'Still a lot of people around town you haven't met. Some of them are keen to keep young men like yourself here.'

'I imagine there are just as many who'll be happy to see me leave.'

'Happen that'll be the way of it in every town in every state. If you mean to stay some place you have to nurture those who share your views and try not to antagonize those who don't.'

'That sounds like good advice, sheriff.'

★  ★  ★

155

The graveside service was short. After the preacher had spoken his last words those congregated circled in the direction of the Galbraith family to give their useless words of condolence. Charlie lingered at the back of the crowd, feeling awkward because he was responsible for the death of one of these men and rejoiced in the fact that Fess Salter had overcome the other one. He had nothing to say that wouldn't be a bare-faced lie. Even so, he stayed where he was, shuffling from one foot to the other because leaving might arouse the suspicions of the sheriff.

Suddenly, an angry voice sounded close at hand, the words flying like razor-sharp arrows and bringing all other conversations to an end.

'Stay away from me. You were told not to come here.'

Charlie stretched up to see over the tops of the closest mourners. Despite her lowered veil and heated words he could still see the paleness of Harriet

Galbraith's face. But there was fire in her dark eyes and Charlie edged forward to catch a glimpse of the subject of her ire. It took only a moment for him to recognize the boyish figure of Clint Revlon.

'Harriet,' Clint said. 'We'll catch whoever is responsible for killing Tom and Wade. They'll be made to pay. You can count on me to protect you.'

'Protect me!' Those words were almost shouted, then she continued with ice in her voice. 'I hold you responsible for the death of my brother. If you hadn't come to Hot Springs he would still be alive. Now go away.'

'You can't believe that I wanted any harm to come to Tom. I was his friend.'

'Go away,' repeated Harriet.

Those gathered near stood in silence. Only Charlie moved, stepping forward so that he came between the adversaries. He faced Clint Revlon. 'It would be good manners to allow the young lady to bury her brother. She's asked you to leave. I suggest you do so.'

Clint Revlon glared at Charlie, his face red but before he could speak two of his comrades took his arms and tried to hustle him away. He shook them off and pointed a finger at Charlie. 'If anyone shouldn't be here it's you. I think you killed Tom Galbraith and when I prove it I'll be looking for you.' He let his hand slap meaningfully against the gun at his side. Charlie saw that it was housed in a new brown holster with an intricate filigree pattern. It was Dave Willis's holster, proving that Clint Revlon had been his assailant in the alleyway at the side of The Cotton Queen.

'This is neither the time nor the place for such talk,' Charlie said. 'Just go.'

Because his friends insisted, Clint allowed them to lead him away from the church.

The sheriff, who had been talking with Harriet's parents when the incident had begun, arrived while Charlie watched Clint Revlon's departure.

'What happened?' asked the sheriff.

'I told Clint Revlon he wasn't wanted here,' said Harriet Galbraith. 'This gentleman simply enforced my wishes.'

The explanation was in keeping with what the sheriff suspected. 'His time would be better spent at home, putting his farm in order and building for the future.'

Charlie said nothing, to his way of thinking Clint Revlon had little future to build for.

Harriet spoke directly to Charlie. 'I believe I owe you an apology,' she said. 'Yesterday I was rude.'

'Not at all,' he said, 'you were rightly shocked by the sight of your brother across his horse.'

'Will you answer a question?' she asked.

'If I'm able.'

'Why did you bring Tom's body here?'

'I hadn't the means to bury them and this was the first town I came across. I didn't want to leave the bodies in the dust, Miss Galbraith. Over the last four years I've seen too many good men on both sides just left to rot where they fell.'

For a moment there was silence then Harriet spoke again. 'We understand you are looking for work, Mr Jefferson.'

'I am.'

'When Tom returned from the fighting he undertook all the heavy work in our mercantile store. We need someone to replace him.'

Once again, Charlie was embarrassed by the situation in which he found himself. It seemed as though the Galbraith family entertained no suspicion that he had been involved in Tom's death. 'I have no experience of that kind of work,' Charlie told her.

'All you need is a strong back and the ability to drive a team of horses.'

He smiled. 'Then I'm perfect for the job, but under the circumstances it might be best to wait a couple of days. Given a bit of time, your parents might think of a more suitable employee.'

Later, as he accompanied the curious sheriff back to Main Street, Charlie thought up a hasty reason for his apparent reluctance to take up the Galbraith family's offer. 'I've always figured store-keeping for a permanent job. I'm not sure that I intend to stay around here too long.'

'Harriet Galbraith is a real pretty girl. Lots of fellows would jump at the chance to be close to her every day.'

Charlie grinned. 'Perhaps that's why I didn't dismiss the idea completely.' Then, more seriously, he asked, 'What's the history between her and the kid I chased away?'

'Clint Revlon? He's hankered after the girl for a year now but she's made it clear that she wants nothing to do with him. When Tom began to mix with him and his friends he seemed to regard it as a licence to press his advances. Harriet's father warned him about his behaviour and for a week or two he's stayed away from her. But he's been a nuisance to the whole town for a year, and more so since Lee's surrender, spending his hours in The Cotton Queen bemoaning injustices to his family instead of applying himself to rebuilding his home.'

'Injustices?'

'His father and brother were killed during the war and his farm was ransacked by Union soldiers.'

'That happened to a lot of people,' said Charlie.

'The lad can't let it go,' the sheriff said.

'Do you think he rides with the Red Masks?'

The sheriff shook his head. 'My understanding is that these bushwhacker bands consist of ex-soldiers. Clint Revlon took no part in the war. He talks a lot and tries to convince people he's a dangerous man but he has no history to back it up.'

Charlie had a different opinion of Clint Revlon; he knew him to be a violent man. He thought of the gunbelt that had belonged to Dave Willis and now hung around Revlon's waist and, too, he remembered the cowardly blows Revlon had delivered while he'd been held by other men. However, before Charlie could make further comment his attention was drawn to a commotion at the far end of the street. He and the sheriff quickened their pace.

Men were shouting and gathering in the middle of the street outside the telegraph office. Dust hung in the air and the boardwalks abounded with inquisitive people.

'What's going on?' called the sheriff, as he and Charlie worked their way through the throng. As men moved aside they could see two horses at the centre of the group.

'Came galloping in, sheriff,' one man said, 'running wild. We had to catch them before someone got hurt.'

The horses were restless, worried by the number of people around them, sensing the agitation of the crowd. Each one was being held by the bridle but most people were concerned with the bundle across each saddle. The bodies were roped securely to the animals but their identities were not easy to discern. A red hood covered each head.

'Get those masks off,' ordered the sheriff and hands set to work immediately to reveal the faces of the dead men.

Charlie knew they were the limper and his friend, other people called out the names of Jake Preston and Slim Halliday. Someone observed that they had been friends of the two whose graves weren't yet filled in.

'Someone's holding a vendetta against the Red Masks,' said a man holding the head of one of the horses.

'Then he's a dead man.' This was Clint Revlon who had come running to the scene with the two men who had led him away from the churchyard. One of them pulled at Clint's arm, warning him to be guarded in his words. Clint dragged his arm free, the anger etched on his face put there as much by his companion's attempt to control him as by the bodies on the horses. 'Didn't anyone see anything?' he yelled.

'They came down from the hill road,' said a man on the boardwalk.

'I think I heard shots,' said his wife. 'Two,' she added, 'in quick succession.'

'Whoever did this chased these horses into town.'

'Then let's get after them.' This was Charlie Jefferson, his eyes meeting those of the hostile Clint Revlon, pretending to be as offended by the violence that had been visited on Hot Springs as much as any other citizen. 'Who's riding with me?' he called as he turned his horse towards the hill trail.

Charlie was playing out the role that he and Fess had planned. By taking the lead in the hunt for the killer of the bushwhackers he hoped to achieve two things. The first aim was to make other gang members believe that he was not their enemy, and the second aim was to lead them away from Fess who was now heading out towards a site near Forster's Bend where he would wait for Charlie.

Without checking who or how many had leapt into their saddles to follow him out of Hot Springs, Charlie rode for the high country. Reaching a vantage point which gave him a commanding view of the country ahead and the trail back to town, he paused and counted eight men in the group behind. He was pleased to see Clint Revlon and his pals among the riders. He waved them forward with urgency, as though he had spotted the quarry and was anxious to end the chase. Further ahead, where the trail looped the hillside, he waited for them to catch up and they divided into three groups to search separate sections of that area. One group, neither the one that Charlie was part of nor the one formed by Clint and his friends, found the place where Fess had previously camped. The tell-tale signs of the shoot-out, chipped boulders, ejected shell cases and blood smears, were clear to see, but by now the day was drawing to a close and they called off the search.

Clint Revlon and his friends hung behind on the journey back to Hot Springs and when they rode into town several minutes behind the main group, Charlie was aware that one of the threesome was missing.

# 10

The killing of the two Red Mask riders and their possible association with Tom Galbraith and Wade Mason was virtually the sole topic of conversation on the streets of Hot Springs the following day. More people acknowledged Charlie Jefferson when they passed him on the street. Several wished him 'Good morning' as he sat on the hotel porch, as did others who saw him outside the telegraph or walking between the two places.

In The Cotton Queen he allowed himself to be drawn into the edges of conversations, expressed views that emphasized his desire for work and money but which were sufficiently indeterminate as to allow those with whom he spoke to draw their own conclusions regarding his political bias. In exchange, it was clear that few people were surprised that the limper and his friend had been members of the Red Mask gang and that, by association, they accepted that Tom Galbraith and Wade Mason had also been members. In hushed tones, one or two wondered what action the sheriff would take against others who were cut from the same cloth but, in general, there was greater concern that the military would descend on Hot Springs and put the town under martial law. There was real fear that the town would suffer for harbouring bushwhackers.

Harriet Galbraith was struggling with a barrel of apples outside the mercantile store when Charlie passed by.

'Allow me,' he said, rolling it into a position that didn't hamper access to the store.

Harriet pushed a strand of fair hair away from her face. Her eyes were blue but so pale that it seemed that the true colour had been drained from them. Even so, they regarded him with such intensity that Charlie thought she knew the role he'd played in her brother's death. In fact, Harriet was confused.

'I was surprised to hear that you led the hunt to catch the killer of the Red Masks,' she began. 'When we spoke yesterday I got the impression that you believed there had been enough killing.'

'I didn't go after them in search of revenge,' he told her, 'but justice. If the dead men tied across their horses had been carpetbaggers or jayhawkers I would have wanted to catch their killers, too, because until all of these people have been stopped there is no chance of reconstruction or prosperity in the south. The bushwhackers claim to be fighting for a cause but that isn't true. The former systems of the southern states cannot be regained, these rebels are raiding, robbing and killing for their own reward and people across the states are suffering at their hands just as much as they are at the hands of the northern profiteers.'

Charlie stopped talking, angry that he'd declared himself an opponent of the bushwhackers but also aware that despite his honesty he was deceiving Harriet Galbraith more than anyone else.

Harriet had absorbed every word he'd spoken and was surprised and excited by his conviction. 'We need men like you around here,' she told him.

Charlie shuffled awkwardly. What he'd said was a true reflection of his belief but he had strayed to this stretch of country hoping to garner enough money to return to the valley of the Tatanka with the fortune he'd promised Ruth Prescott. 'I won't be staying here long,' he told Harriet. 'It wouldn't be right to take the job you offered me. You need someone permanent and I guess I'm not him.'

Harriet's mouth opened a little way as though there were many words she wanted to say but none came out.

'My home is in the Wyoming Territory,' Charlie continued, 'and I'll be heading that way soon.'

'Do you have a wife there?'

The question surprised Charlie and he could see by her sudden change of expression that Harriet Galbraith had shocked herself by asking it. 'No,' he said, but the twist of his lips betrayed the truth of the matter to Harriet, that there was a girl out west who awaited his return.

'Will I see you before you leave?' Harriet asked.

'I should be around for a few more days,' he told her, but in that he was wrong.

\* \* \*

The manner of Charlie's abduction later that night was almost identical to the method adopted two nights earlier, but this time no one threw a blanket over his head and no one drove their fist into the pit of his stomach. Within a dozen strides of leaving The Cotton Queen he found himself flanked by two hooded men who directed him into a gap between buildings which Charlie suspected was the same place he'd been dragged into previously. Charlie resisted only slightly. Although there was no sign of un-holstered weapons he assumed the men would brook no refusal.

'What do you want?' he asked.

No one replied. Instead he was pushed ahead and two other hooded figures emerged from the shadows, closing off any means of escape. One of the newcomers was in constant motion, his weight shifted from one foot to the other and his right hand rested on the butt of his pistol as though not pulling it and pointing it at Charlie was a struggle against the law of nature.

Charlie recognized the holster and was tempted to address Clint Revlon by name but he was aware that revealing his cleverness might also seal his fate. These men were capable of killing to protect their identities. 'What do you want?' he asked again.

'Could be we want to offer you a job,' said one of the men. 'Word around town is that you are looking for quick money. Perhaps we can help.'

'Why would you want to help me?'

'You took off after the killer of our friends like a man on a mission,' the spokesman said. 'We know you were a soldier and perhaps, like us, you don't want to see those from the north getting rich at our expense.'

Without being able to see the faces of the men around him it was impossible for Charlie to determine the level of sincerity behind the words. It could be that the man spoke with a sneer on his lips, that somehow he had learned that Charlie had fought for the Union during the war and still served the government, but if his attempts to delude the bushwhackers were bearing fruit then he now had the opportunity to get closer to the gang. He recalled that one of Clint's friends had not returned to Hot Springs after yesterday's wild goose chase after Fess and wondered if he had ridden on to Pottersville to consult with the boss. Perhaps they were seeking replacements for the four men they had lost.

Ironically, it was Clint Revlon, speaking out against the spokesman's proposal, who gave Charlie the belief that he had been accepted by the other Red Masks.

'I don't trust him.' Clint's tone was heavy with petulance, a carry-over, Charlie assumed, from the confrontation at the cemetery.

'It's got nothing to do with you,' the spokesman told him, 'the boss will decide.'

'Who is the boss?' asked Charlie.

'Come with us tonight and you'll meet him tomorrow.'

Charlie had no choice. If he refused to go with them they would probably kill him here in the alley, but if he left now he wouldn't have the opportunity to contact Fess Salter.

'Well?' asked the spokesman, the one word heavy with impatience.

Clint Revlon's hand hitched on his gun butt to add his own demand for urgency.

'No harm in talking,' said Charlie keeping his tone even, as though responding to nothing more sinister than Harriet Galbraith's offer to work in the mercantile store.

The spokesman led the way out of the alley to the rear of the buildings on Main Street where five horses were saddled and waiting. Charlie was surprised to find that one of them was his own. Refusing to ride with the bushwhackers had not been an option.

When they were clear of town the men removed their hoods. Charlie wasn't surprised to find that the men with Clint Revlon were the same as those who had been with him at Tom Galbraith's funeral. Little was said during the long ride and Charlie's twice-asked request for their destination was ignored.

Shortly before dawn, when the night had lost the full density of blackness but before the pink fingers of a new day's sun had begun to stretch across the territory, they paused on a bluff. In such darkness, the features of the men around Charlie were indiscernible, the figures merely silhouettes and the landscape indistinguishable. Yet, strangely, he was gripped by the sensation that he knew this place. For a moment he wondered if they had been riding in circles — if, in fact, they were in the high ground where Fess had encamped earlier.

When they reached the valley floor he knew that this was not the case. They had swung back into the jaws of a canyon and were heading towards a collection of low buildings that were almost indistinguishable in the dim light. At a fence they paused while one of the riders unhooked the iron loop that held the gate closed. Charlie scrutinized the gate post and found the spot where a splinter had recently been gouged out. He was back at the farm where the woman had refused him water. That day she had recognized him as a Union soldier, if she did so again he would be dead before the sun rose over the horizon.

It was clear that Max, the man who had done the talking in the alley, was the acknowledged leader of the group. When they'd dismounted outside the rundown building that was the farmhouse he told Denny, a wiry fellow with sunken cheeks and a long, bristle-covered jaw, to see to the horses. Without complaint, Denny led all five hoses away while the others went into the house.

'Saw you coming,' the woman greeted them as though needing to make it clear why they hadn't been challenged or shot at when they came through the yard gate. 'Got word from Pottersville to expect you. Coffee's bubbling on the stove. Give me ten minutes and I'll serve up breakfast.'

'Ten minutes is too long, Ma,' said Clint Revlon. If there was meant to be humour in the remark, it didn't carry.

'Speak to me like that again and I'll crack the skillet over your head,' she told him.

Max glared at Clint. 'Your ma is close to being the only friend you have right now,' he told the younger man. 'If I was you I wouldn't go upsetting her.'

It hadn't escaped Charlie's notice that Clint was only tolerated by the other Red Mask members. In Pottersville, when Mort Goudry had thrown him out of his saloon, Tom Galbraith and Wade Mason had scarce been able to hide their scorn for the young man, while in Hot Springs those in his company treated him like a kid brother they'd been lumbered with when they had money enough in their pockets to spend a wet afternoon in the nearest bordello. Now Max had made it clear: the boy was unpopular.

Max had also made clear the fact that this was Clint's home and the abrasive woman was his mother. This was also a meeting place for the Red Masks and, Charlie supposed, more than that. He recalled the large string of horses he had seen from the bluff some days earlier and how incongruous they had appeared on the run-down farm. Now he knew them to be re-mounts for the bushwhacker gang, rested and fed for the next raid.

To Charlie's relief, the woman busied herself preparing the food and spared him not a single glance. Nonetheless, he kept his hat low on his brow to give her little to see if she did glance his way and hoped that his presence with the other bushwhackers was sufficient to allay any suspicion that might later arise.

Max ordered Silas, the other gang member, out to the corral to help Denny. 'Two of you should get the horses unsaddled and watered in ten minutes. Breakfast will be ready when you get back.'

Silas didn't argue but threw a look in Clint's direction as if to say that the kid should be doing the job. However, his expression changed as though acknowledging that it would take longer or wouldn't get done properly if the task was left in Clint's hands.

'Who's this then?' asked the woman when she brought bread to the table where Charlie and Max were sitting. 'New member?'

'He's here to meet the boss.'

With a searching expression the woman looked at Charlie and seemed, for a moment, to pause. Their eyes met and held. Charlie thought there was nothing to be gained by avoiding the look. If she thought she recognized him the only thing he could do was bluff it out.

'Something wrong?' he asked.

She shook her head. 'I guess not,' she replied.

Clint spoke up. 'I don't trust him,' he told the woman.

'That's because I had to teach you some manners at the graveside,' Charlie told him, happy enough to antagonize the boy.

'Quit it,' ordered Max, his voice quiet because he was accustomed to instant obedience.

'Pestering a girl at her brother's

funeral, you're lucky I didn't slap you senseless.'

Clint's hand reached for his pistol.

'Get your hand away from that gun,' shouted Max. 'He's right. You should have been knocked senseless for drawing attention to us.'

The woman slammed her hand on the table. 'This is my house and I won't have talk from anyone about harming my son. I'll shoot anyone who touches him.' Her eyes slid to the corner behind the door where the two Hall single-shot rifles were propped against the wall.

Max wasn't prepared to have his authority challenged by a woman, even if he was in her home.

'Your boy's in trouble with the boss,' he told her. 'I don't think he'll let him ride with us anymore.'

The woman was taken aback. 'What's he done?'

'I expect the boss will tell you when he gets here.'

Heavy noises sounded beyond the door, the sounds of a struggle, someone falling on the planks of the porch then bouncing against the wall of the house. A hoarse voice yelled a warning then the door burst open and a figure was propelled into the room. Behind came Denny and Silas. Silas held a pistol in his hand and pointed it at the figure now lying on the floor, at the feet of those gathered at the table for a meal.

'Caught this one prowling in the yard,' said Silas, 'sneaking up on Denny.'

The man rubbed the back of his head as he sat up. 'I wasn't prowling,' he grumbled, 'just looking to bed down in your barn for the night. Lost my horse up there on the bluff and saw your light down below. Didn't see the man in the corral. I was walking quietly so that I didn't disturb anyone in the house.'

'That ain't true,' snapped Silas, 'he saw Denny OK. Was watching him unsaddle the horses when I came up behind him.

'Sure,' the man said, 'when I got close to the corral I heard the fellow talking to the beasts but by then I was so close that I figured if I called out I might durn near scare him to death. So I planned on waiting until he'd finished before grabbing a few hours sleep in the barn. I'd have come knocking at the house door at sun-up. In my experience a stranger in daylight is always less threatening than one who arrives in the dark.'

While he spoke, the man looked from face to face of those gathered around. When he reached Charlie Jefferson he allowed no change in his expression or tone, did nothing to betray the fact that they were associated. Charlie Jefferson acted in similar fashion but he knew that Fess Salter's arrival at this time would raise the possibility that they had been followed from Hot Springs which would, in turn, increase any suspicious thought that the bushwhackers held about his own role in recent events.

'Are you looking for Clint Revlon?' Max asked Fess.

'Who?'

'Clint Revlon. Heard tell that a man fitting your description was looking for Clint in Pottersville.'

'Not me,' said Fess. 'I'm not looking for anyone, just heading for Texas.'

Clint had drawn his revolver and was doing those dancing steps that he did whenever he was agitated. 'I don't trust him,' he told Max. 'I don't trust either of them. I say we kill them now.'

'Shut up, Clint,' ordered Max. 'Go and help your mother.' Max's words were meant to be insulting and when Denny and Silas grinned the youngster turned red. 'We'll let the boss decide when he gets here.'

# 11

During the remainder of the morning no opportunity arose for Charlie and Fess to communicate. Fess was roped and led out to the barn to await the arrival of the boss and Charlie knew that manufacturing any sort of excuse to leave the house and head in that direction would only increase any suspicion already harboured against him. He was grateful that his side-arm had not been taken from him but as the morning progressed its value diminished.

Shortly after day-break, men began to assemble at the house and by late morning the group was thirty strong. Eggs, bacon and flapjacks were prepared for many of them and the coffee pot was constantly refilled. Most of the men lingered in the yard because there were too many for the house, thereby rendering hopeless any plan that Charlie cherished for the rescue of Fess.

It was late in the morning when Denny came into the house with the news. 'The boss is here.'

The woman was the first to move, stepping over the threshold to meet him on the porch but not with words of greeting. Charlie, who remained seated, heard the anger in the woman's voice as her words tumbled out unchecked.

'We have an agreement,' she said. 'I let you use my home as your headquarters and in return you take my boy on your raids. He wants to avenge his father and brother and is as anxious to continue the fight against the north as any of these other men who wear a red hood.'

The man backed into the room, throwing back words against the woman's unexpected attack.

'Your son dropped his hood in a Pottersville alley. If, as Sheriff Bland anticipated, the finding of it had been an indication that we were about to raid that town, the whole gang might have been wiped out. As it is, his unguarded tongue has attracted the attention of Union spies and as a result four of my men have been needlessly killed. Clint isn't trusted by these men and I won't let him put our plans in jeopardy.'

The woman continued to defend her son, demanded proof of the charges against him. 'I've kept my part of the bargain,' she said. 'I've fed these men and those horses in the corral. When you raid Arkadelphia tonight then Clint has to ride with you. We need his share of the money. You owe me that much.'

'You'll get your money,' the man replied, turning now so that finally Charlie could see his face. Mort Goudry looked Charlie squarely in the eyes. 'You the new man?'

'That's right,' said Charlie.

'I've seen you before. In Pottersville.'

Charlie agreed. He remembered Mort Goudry throwing Clint Revlon into the street. At the time he'd assumed that that had been done because the saloon keeper feared that Clint's anti-government rants might lead to a fight and damage to his premises, but now it was clear that he had been deflecting suspicion, making it appear that he embraced the new peace.

'You were with two brothers,' continued Mort Goudry, his memory edging his conversation with caution. 'They were ex-Union soldiers.'

'I believe they were,' Charlie told him.

'Union?' This was Max.

'The war's over,' Charlie told him. 'I wasn't looking to start it up again.'

Max wasn't satisfied. Neither was Mort Goudry. 'You were a Union soldier, too,' he said. 'I remember that military holster you wore.'

Everyone in the room fell silent. All eyes were fixed on Charlie.

'Now I know him,' said the woman. 'Came riding by here some days back. I chased him off with my rifle. Should have put the bullet in him not the gate post.'

'I told you all along I didn't trust him,' chimed in Clint. 'And I'll bet he's in cahoots with that other fellow.'

'What other fellow?' asked Mort.

Max told him about Fess locked up in the barn. 'He might be the one who claimed he was looking for Clint in the Wild Horse. Figure you'd be able to identify him.'

'I haven't seen him before,' Clint announced as though that would dispel any responsibility for being tracked down by Union spies.

Mort Goudry ignored him and he and Max headed off to the barn. When they returned it was clear Fess had been identified as the man who had ridden out of Pottersville with Tom Galbraith and Wade Mason.

When Mort began issuing orders to his lieutenants it became apparent to Charlie that the saloon owner would take no part in the raid. He ordered them to attack at midnight and named the targets which would yield the most money. There was the bank at one end of North Street, Saville's Emporium at the other end, and the three saloons between. 'Come back here to change horses then scatter. This will be the last raid for a while,' he told them. 'The authorities are getting too close. I'll be in touch when the time is right to ride again.'

'What about him?' Max asked, inclining his head towards Charlie.

'Leave someone behind to take care of him and the other one.'

'I'll do it.' All eyes turned towards the speaker, Clint Revlon. Already his gun was in his hand as if prepared to execute Charlie in the confined space of the house.

'I want it handled by someone I can trust,' Goudry said.

'You can trust my boy,' snapped the woman. 'You won't let him ride with you so let him show you what he can do.' When Goudry hesitated she spoke again. 'I've got two rifles over there that will blow a hole clean through a man. There won't be any mistakes.'

Goudry spoke to Max. 'Leave someone here to make sure the job gets done. They need to be taken up into the hills or somewhere away from the regular trails. I don't want their bones ever to be found.'

* * *

It was late afternoon when a disgruntled Denny stood in the yard watching the diminishing dust cloud of the departed riders. He walked over to the corral, selected four horses and set about the task of preparing them for a journey into the high ground.

Inside the house, Charlie knew that if he failed to turn the tables on Clint Revlon and his mother, he would be dead within an hour. When he'd been identified as a government spy his gun had been taken but, because of the overwhelming odds against him, no one had bothered to bind him. Now he stood, threw a meaningful glance in the direction of his pistol which lay with

Fess Salter's on top of a rugged chest of drawers, and began to shuffle slowly in that direction.

Clint drew his pistol and motioned for Charlie to move backwards towards the other side of the room. 'I can kill you here and tote your body out to the wastelands,' he said. 'It's all the same to me.'

'Still trying to convince yourself that you're a man,' said Charlie, 'but they've left a nursemaid behind in case you haven't the nerve for the job.' He threw a glance over his shoulder, towards the window, as though able to see Denny at work in the yard.

'Shut up,' said Clint.

'My boy is man enough for the job,' the woman said, 'just like his pa and brother were when they went to war.'

'I've never met a mother so anxious for the death of her son,' Charlie said. 'That's what's going to happen, Clint. If I don't kill you I reckon they'll hang you for treason. I don't see you going down in a hail of bullets when the army gets here. I think you'll throw down your gun and beg for mercy. Won't do you any good. They'll stand you on a trapdoor with a rope around your neck.'

'Shut up,' Clint shouted and again waved his pistol to warn Charlie not to try for the pistols that his eyes had once more rested upon.

Charlie held up his hands as if imploring Clint not to fire and he edged backwards again, further into the corner behind the door.

'Of course,' he said, 'I don't care if you are a Red Mask or if you want the Confederacy to rise again or if you are seeking vengeance for the death of your kinfolk. I want you for murder. You killed two young men while they slept. That's murder in every state.'

For a moment there was silence, Clint and his mother unsure why their prisoner was acting with such confidence.

Then Clint spoke, the sneer with which he hoped to adorn his words less prominent than usual. 'They were Union soldiers.'

Charlie took another step back, his right hand, hidden from their sight, reaching behind. 'They weren't soldiers,' he said, 'they were civilians. You might not be in favour of Lee's surrender but nonetheless it stands. The war is over. You murdered Dave and Henry Willis on the banks of the Ouachita and I know that is true because you are wearing Dave's gun-belt.'

Charlie pointed at the brown leather belt around Clint's waist, distracting the younger man long enough to be able to pull forward the Hall single-shot rifle that his right hand had grasped. The woman gasped when she saw that Charlie was armed and the sound of her surprise caused Clint to raise his head. He, too, saw that he had been caught off-guard by Charlie's chatter and movement but it was too late to save his life. Charlie pulled the trigger and proved the validity of the woman's claim. The force of the bullet which smashed into the centre of Clint's body lifted him off his feet and threw him headlong against the far wall. The woman screamed and moved towards her dead son. Charlie moved more quickly, grabbed her by the arm and flung her against the wall to prevent her reaching any of the weapons that were in the room. She was a venomous woman and would, he knew, kill him if the means was within her grasp.

He pushed his pistol into its holster, tucked the guns of Fess Salter and Clint Revlon into his waist band. He snatched the other Hall rifle from its position in the corner and had it in his hands when he opened the door. Although much of the sound of the gunshot would have been contained within the house, Charlie still knew that the reverberations would have carried to Denny in the corral. He was right, as he walked out on to the porch Denny bustled around the corner wondering, no doubt, what calamity had been wrought by Clint Revlon. When he saw Charlie, he stopped.

'Throw down your gun,' Charlie shouted.

Denny cast a glance towards the barn, his thoughts easy to understand. Not only did the barn provide protection but Fess Salter was imprisoned there and could, perhaps, be used as a bargaining chip. He moved, his left knee bending in the direction of his hoped-for sanctuary while his right hand began to pull his pistol free from its holster. He fired one shot but it was wild and didn't trouble Charlie. Charlie fired one shot and Denny was thrown like an unwanted scarecrow back towards the corral.

Knowing the range of the old rifle, Charlie smashed its stock against the house wall to ensure it couldn't be re-loaded and used by the woman as soon as he rode away. He collected the other rifle from the house and gave it the same treatment.

The woman was weeping over her

dead son but there was loathing in her eyes for Charlie.

'I hope you are satisfied,' he said. 'The army will soon be here. I expect they'll take you away and try you for treason.' Then he left her.

While cutting Fess free from his bindings, the older man recounted the events which had led him to this place. Worried that Charlie's plan to delude the bushwhackers had failed, he'd arrived in Hot Springs under cover of darkness and had witnessed Charlie's abduction from outside The Cotton Queen. Fess had waited at the mouth of the alley ready to intervene if Charlie's life was threatened and had stayed as close as possible when he'd left town in company with the Red Mask riders.

Charlie told Fess all he knew and added that they needed to contact Colonel Crook at Fort Smith.

'There might not be time to get soldiers to the town but a telegraph message from him would give them the chance to prepare an ambush.'

Fort Smith was more than a hundred miles north of their current location thus, with time a critical factor, a telegraph message was Fess Salter's only method of communication with the colonel. Using the telegraph office in Hot Springs might bring him to the attention of the sheriff but it was the nearest and he carried credentials to prove that he was on government business, so it was agreed that he would make Hot Springs his destination.

'I'll ride directly to Arkadelphia to lend my gun to the fighting,' Charlie said. 'If the town is properly organized then we can break this gang of bushwhackers forever.'

# 12

Arkadelphia was more than twenty miles away on the banks of the Ouachita. Charlie figured that by mixing the speeds of his horse, a steady gallop, a loping canter, and now and then slowing to a walk, he could conserve the animal's strength but still cover the distance in a little more than two hours. Before heading south he contemplated riding to Pottersville to arrest Mort Goudry but the gang leader was not aware that his plan was in danger of failure so there would be time enough to bring him to justice after the gang had been smashed.

It occurred to him that the Red Masks had been no more than an hour ahead when he left the farm and he had no way of knowing their speed. Caution was required; he didn't want to ride into their midst. They would have chosen a place to wait until dark but no doubt it would be a location from which they could observe travellers on the trail. He knew they were going to split into two groups and enter the town from each end but he guessed that they would stay together until the raid began.

When he reached the river he was still several miles from the town but the closer he got the more likely it became that he might be seen and recognized. His gut feeling was that the bushwhackers would have stayed on the western side of the river so he gambled, found a suitable ford and crossed to the eastern bank. If, in the gloom, a sharp-eyed gang member had seen him then it was likely that the raid would be abandoned, but he'd reduced the risk of capture and all else was a chance he had to take.

Once across the river he pushed on quickly towards Arkadelphia, hoping that the authorities there had already received a message from Colonel

Crook. When he rode into town there was no activity of the kind he expected to see. North Street ran parallel with the river and Charlie's first impression was that it would be difficult to trap the raiders here. Side streets and alleys were abundant and at its centre and dividing the street was an open square, across which the stone built town hall and law court faced each other.

Charlie dismounted outside the town hall and tried the door. It seemed likely that the town council would be discussing the message from the army and making plans to defend their town. The door, however, was locked and no lights shone from within. Swiftly, Charlie dashed along North Street, grabbed the arm of a citizen and asked for directions to the sheriff's office.

A deputy drinking coffee was writing in a ledger when Charlie opened the door.

'I'm looking for the sheriff,' he said.

The deputy waved his arm in a

gesture of indifference. 'He's somewhere around town,' was the answer. 'He'll be back in half an hour.'

'Find him,' Charlie ordered, 'we haven't got half an hour to waste. This town is going to be attacked by the Red Masks tonight. You've got to assemble a posse to protect the place.'

The deputy's mouth gaped, unsure how much credence he should give to the stranger's outrageous announcement. 'Who are you?'

'My name is Charlie Jefferson. I'm a government agent and you need to act swiftly.' When the deputy hesitated, Charlie pulled him from his chair. 'Come on,' he said, 'we'll find the sheriff together.'

Without any option the deputy led the way out of the office. He headed back towards the square and Charlie wondered if the lawman was in the town hall as he had suspected when he'd first arrived in Arkadelphia. But that wasn't their destination. They passed the central square and entered the foyer of Buckman's Hotel. A clerk was sitting in a slowly rocking chair reading a newspaper. Surprise filled his eyes when he saw the deputy.

'Is he here?' the deputy asked.

The clerk made a point of looking at the wall clock. 'Usually is at this time,' he said, 'hope you're not thinking of disturbing him.'

'Which room?'

'Same as usual. Number seven.'

The deputy led the way up the red carpeted stairs with Charlie close behind. The word seven had been stencilled on the bedroom door with gold-coloured paint. Grunts, giggles, slaps and moans sounded at the other side of the door. The deputy raised his hand to knock, paused and cast a look at Charlie. 'I hope this isn't some sick joke, mister, because the sheriff isn't going to take this well.'

Charlie thumped on the door with his fist and evoked a string of curse words from the other side.

'Sheriff,' said the deputy, 'it's Bob.

You are needed.'

'I'm needed in here.'

'It's important. An emergency.'

'If you value your job, Bob, you'll go away now. I'll be back in the office in a few minutes.'

Charlie grasped the handle of the door and pushed. It was locked so, using his shoulder to good effect, he barged the door with such velocity as to wrench the bolt from the inside doorpost.

'What the hell?' shouted the sheriff and his words were accompanied by a high-pitched shriek.

'Sorry for the interruption, sheriff, but this is important and there's no time to lose.'

'Who are you?' yelled the sheriff as he grabbed a blanket off the bed which left the other occupant deprived of any cover for her modesty. But the initial surprise at Charlie's abrupt entrance had passed for her and she giggled as she watched the sheriff struggling to achieve a combination of outrage and modesty.

'I'm a government agent and your town is about to be visited by the Red Mask gang. You should have had a message to that effect from Colonel Crook at Fort Smith.'

Pulling on his britches the sheriff denied that any such communication had been received. 'The telegraph office is closed for the day,' he said.

'Then you'll have to take my word for it and make a plan to trap these men.'

'I don't have to do anything you tell me,' said the sheriff, still angered by the rude interruption. 'But I guess I'll speak to the mayor.'

'What do I tell my husband about the broken lock?' asked the girl.

'Tell him the truth,' said the sheriff, 'that a madman burst into your room. Or else get it fixed before he returns.' With his clothing still in disarray he quit the room with Charlie and the deputy close behind.

The mayor was at home playing checkers on the porch with the doctor while their wives gossiped and sewed indoors. The men listened, incredulous of the sheriff's words, the Red Masks could have no reason to raid their town which had been loyal to the Confederate cause to the very end.

Charlie urged them to act and eventually the mayor agreed.

'Let's get the council together as quickly as possible and formulate a plan of action,' he announced. 'Sheriff, get Al to open the telegraph office and find out if this message from the army is true or a figment of this fellow's imagination.'

Charlie wasn't pleased to have his word doubted nor, he thought, was this a time for democracy. This was a time for action not words, and councilmen in his experience always possessed too much of the latter and too little of the former. He pressed upon the mayor the urgency of the situation.

His reluctance to have the matter placed before the good men of Arkadelphia was well-founded. Following the mayor's explanation for the extraordinary meeting, every man gathered there had a point of view that they wanted to express and the assembly swiftly became a rabble as each man argued with his neighbour.

'Gentlemen,' Charlie shouted, desperate to restore calm and urge the men to action, 'I know that I'm a stranger to all of you but I implore you to set to work defending your town. There is little time left to save it from the fate that befell Pine Bluff recently. I know that some of you have sympathy with what you believe to be the cause of the Red Masks but that is a myth. This gang is intent on robbery and destruction. They are not freedom fighters, just common criminals. They must be stopped and if it is not done here they will continue to burn and pillage all over Arkansas. You need to rouse every able man in the town to destroy this gang tonight.'

'Mr Jefferson is right,' said the mayor, 'we must organise ourselves into an effective posse.'

'What if they don't come?' someone asked.

'If they don't come we've lost a night's sleep and I'll charge this fellow with wasting our time,' the mayor replied, 'but if they do come and we don't do anything then how do we face our families in the morning and every day after that?'

The mumbling that filled the assembly room proved that the mayor's words were effective and when, at that moment, Bob the deputy entered waving a piece of paper, the committee men were totally swayed.

'Here it is,' said Bob, 'just like Charlie Jefferson said, a message from Fort Smith warning us that we're likely to be hit tonight by the Red Mask gang.'

The sheriff already had a list of men he could rely upon in an emergency and he and all his deputies set about summoning them from their homes and selecting positions along North Street which would put the expected raiders under their guns. Other men, including the town councillors, were gathering boxes, hay bales and anything suitable to form barricades that would seal off exits from the main thoroughfare, and wagons were positioned at either end ready to be rolled across the street after the Red Masks had entered the town. Men heaving and straining in the dim glow of the street lanterns created an eerie spectacle. They worked silently, the prospect of the coming fight robbing them of conversation.

Charlie worked as hard as any man, helping to erect barricades up and down the street. The centre square, he knew, was the weak point. The main targets of the raid, the bank and Saville's emporium, couldn't be seen from the court house or the town hall so there was no value in putting riflemen at either location, and the square itself was too wide for makeshift barricades to be anything but a mild hindrance to a horseman determined to breach them and gain freedom via the side streets and alleys beyond.

Men were sited on roofs all along North Street but there was a concentration of marksmen around the bank and the emporium. Other men lurked behind the side street barricades, their job to cause confusion when the trap was sprung and the raiders attempted to make a break for freedom. Charlie Jefferson stayed at ground level, crouched behind a water trough across the street from the bank. The sheriff was at the other end of the street and it was he who ordered the street lanterns to be extinguished when everyone was in position.

\* \* \*

The defenders of Arkadelphia had expected the raiders to come riproaring into town, filling the citizens with fear for their lives and property. That had been the manner of previous raids throughout the southern states so that the identity of the raiders was not in doubt, nor was the purpose of their visit. This time it was different, which added weight to Charlie's argument that this attack had no political motivation, that this attack was the work of common criminals.

The first sighting of the raiders was made by a townsman on the roof of a rooming house overlooking the bank. They were approaching slowly, the horses kept at walking pace to suppress the sound of their advance, but it was the glow from the firebrands carried by some of the riders which pinpointed their location. They maintained silence until they were at the edge of town where they paused for several moments. As Charlie Jefferson had suspected, the raiders had split into two groups and it wasn't until the flames carried by the second group appeared at the opposite end of North Street that the first group continued their advance.

Most of the group reined their horses to a halt outside the bank while those one or two who had been chosen to break into the saloons progressed farther along the street. It was at that moment, as some of the riders were in the process of dismounting, that Bob, the deputy yelled an order for them to surrender.

'It's a trap,' one of the raiders yelled and he fired his gun in the direction of the deputy's voice.

That was the signal for the men on the roof tops to begin firing. The men in the red hoods were engulfed by the fusillade. Men yelled in agony and horses screamed with pain and fear. Some of the riders were knocked from their saddle while others turned their horses with the intention of riding back out of town.

By now, the wagons that had been held in readiness were being dragged across the top of the street to close the trap on the raiders. Marksmen took their places behind those wagons and poured more bullets into the group of raiders who were made easier targets due to the fact that the only light in the street was shed by the firebrands which they carried.

The bodies of six or seven dead or dying men lay in the street close to the bank. Those raiders that were still mounted were desperately seeking an avenue of escape. Now that they realized they couldn't return the way they had entered the town they were looking for a route along the side streets but it soon became apparent to them that they offered no sanctuary. They came up against guarded barricades at every turn.

Charlie Jefferson left the safety of the water trough and began running towards the town square which he knew offered the raiders the best chance of escape. A bullet flew past his head and smacked into the wall of the building behind. He wasn't sure if the shot had been fired by a Red Mask rider or if it was a stray bullet fired by one of the citizens on the roof. He ran on, pistol in hand. A rider, one of those despatched to rob a saloon, was racing towards him. Charlie didn't know if the man was returning to help his comrades or if he was riding for freedom unaware that the end of the street had been closed off. Charlie stepped into the street, levelled his weapon and pulled the trigger. The hooded man yelled in pain, threw up his arms and tumbled from the back of his horse. When he didn't move again, Charlie ran on.

The sound of battle reached him from the other end of the street but, mixed with the gunfire and the cries of shot men, other anxious voices could be heard. Charlie feared that the trap at the far end of North Street had been less successful.

'Hold them,' he heard someone shout and suspected it was the sheriff.

'There are more coming,' someone replied, and Charlie could hear the sound of galloping horses approaching from the north.

There was little light now and dust mingled with gunsmoke as he dashed onwards to lend his gun to the battle.

Suddenly, a loud cheer punctuated the gunfire: a victory shout, Charlie surmised, and he thought he caught the word 'army'. The additional horsemen had entered the town and they brought with them a metallic rattle which had nothing to do with horse harnesses. Within moments the fighting was finished, the street lights were lit and hoods were being removed to check for survivors of the ambush.

Charlie found Fess Salter with Captain Jessop, who still held his unsheathed sabre in his hand.

'I remembered the captain telling us he was going to the temporary camp at Benton. I wasn't sure he would still be there but after I'd sent the telegraph message to Fort Smith it seemed worth taking a gamble.'

'We were pleased to see you boys,' the sheriff told Captain Jessop. 'The fight began at the other end of the street before we got the wagons in place. The raiders realized it was a trap and were trying to force their way out of town when you arrived. For a dreadful moment we thought you were more Red Masks. It was a relief to see those blue uniforms.'

# 13

When the gunsmoke had cleared, when lamps had been filled with oil, lit and hung on every available peg and nail, the carnage that had taken place on North Street, Arkadelphia was laid bare. Of the twenty-six masked raiders who had ridden into town, twenty-three were dead in the street and two of the remaining three were so badly injured that neither would see the rising of the morning sun. Six horses had to be destroyed and there was no shortage of volunteers to undertake that task, the bloodlust of the citizens still running high in the wake of those few minutes of relentless slaughter.

Up and down the street, groups of men congratulated each other in order to boast of their own exploits, and those three or four who, following the battle, had needed the doctor's attention, displayed their bandages as if they had been decorated with their nation's highest honour. By the end of the day, when the heat of battle had passed away, in keeping with survivors of all bloody encounters, most of them would never want to speak again of what had happened in their town.

Only one townsman, the blacksmith's assistant, had been severely wounded, a gut shot from which it was rumoured that he might not recover.

At the town's expense, the eating houses along North Street kept the men supplied with coffee and victuals but the mayor refused a request for the saloons to serve alcohol on the grounds that there was too much work to do. The street had to be cleared of dead men and all the barricades that had been erected earlier had now to be dismantled so that in the morning the town would function normally.

A reporter of the *Arkadelphia Gazette* pestered the mayor, the sheriff and Captain Jessop for details of the operation that had led to the demise of the Red Mask gang but was brushed aside while they attended to their own necessary functions. Consequently, in the immediate aftermath, he was forced to garner facts and figures from those standing on the street, who might or might not have been involved in the action. His immediate aim was to get enough information to produce a special news-sheet for sale in the morning and to be able to spread details of the town's great victory across the states and all the way to Washington. To that end, the town's telegrapher kept the office open but, until the onset of normal business hours, he was permitted to send only those messages approved by the mayor.

At his earliest opportunity, one of those messages was sent by Captain Jessop to Fort Smith. Although outwardly the captain had maintained an attitude of professional calm since the last shot had been fired, inwardly he was delighted to have reached Arkadelphia in time to be involved in the fight. Being instrumental in ending the raids of a gang like the Red Masks not only sent a message to other bushwhacker groups that the army was determined to wipe them out but it did his personal career no harm whatsoever.

Later, as they drank coffee, Charlie Jefferson, Fess Salter and Captain Jessop planned their next move. Charlie told the officer about the Revlon farm, its function as a meeting place for the gang and the participation of the woman they would find there.

'The gang leader is Mort Goudry,' he added. 'He runs the Wild Horse Saloon in Pottersville.'

'When the men and animals are rested we'll ride over there and arrest him,' decided Captain Jessop.

'It might be best if Fess and I do that,' Charlie told him. 'People hereabouts are wary of the army. They fear martial law, Captain. Fess and I will do the job without too much of a ruckus.'

'Do you know how many men he has with him?'

'Shouldn't think he has any, it was probably his full force that he launched against Arkadelphia. Besides, he didn't encourage the gang members to hang around Pottersville in case they drew attention to him. Fess and I will leave at first light. Goudry has no reason to suppose that the raid has failed so he'll be in his saloon preparing for another day of business. We'll catch him unawares and get him out of town quickly. We'll meet up with you at the Revlon farm. If we aren't there by midday then you know that something has gone wrong and it'll be up to you to catch him.'

* * *

Shortly after dawn, Fess and Charlie set out to arrest Mort Goudry. They reached Pottersville at a time when the town should be settling into its normal daily activities but they were surprised to see clusters of citizens on the street engaged in noisy conversations. One group was stationed outside the Wild Horse Saloon and when Charlie and Fess dismounted and mingled among the men they discovered the reason for the celebration.

'Are you sure about this, Sam Dane?' a voice shouted out.

The man who had recently tacked a poster to the wall of the saloon answered with a decisive head movement. 'Word came over the telegraph less than an hour ago. I confirmed the facts with the mayor of Arkadelphia before printing these handbills. And before you ask, I know nothing else. I hope to include the full story in the next edition of the *Bugle*.'

Numerous questions were thrown at Sam Dane as he pushed his way through the crowd to post the news at another part of town but he answered no one. A glance at the notice was enough to convince Charlie and Fess that their hopes of catching Mort Goudry off guard were now shattered. In letters almost three inches high the banner announced: RED MASK GANG DESTROYED AT ARKADELPHIA.

The tall doors of the Wild Horse Saloon were closed but unlocked. Charlie led the way inside with Fess close on his heels. Ceasing his work with a mop, a swamper told them the place wasn't yet open for business.

'We're looking for Mort Goudry,' declared Charlie.

'Like I told you already, we're not serving yet.' The fellow was weedy thin but belligerent.

'We're not here for whiskey,' Fess told him while pulling his pistol free from its holster.

Charlie looked at the upstairs balcony but there was no movement and all the doors he could see were closed. At the far end of the long counter a door to a rear room was set in an arched recess. With long strides, Charlie made his way in that direction.

'Where do you think you're going?' asked the swamper.

'Is Goudry in there?' asked Charlie.

The other protested loudly. 'You can't go back there.'

Charlie ignored him and proceeded towards the far door.

Suddenly, the swamper swung the long-handled mop at Charlie's head. Although surprised by the man's attack, Charlie easily avoided the blow by ducking low so that the stick passed harmlessly over his head. Before the man was able to regain his balance to try again, Fess intervened. Using his left hand he grasped the pole to thwart its use as a weapon while at the same time he swiped his right hand across the swamper's face. Because Fess still held his pistol in his right hand the blow staggered the man, causing him to release his hold on the mop and fall to the floor.

The man wasn't hurt. He scrambled to his feet and ran towards the street door causing a commotion as he stumbled through it and into the men still gathered outside.

Charlie Jefferson reached the door in the recess and pushed it open. Mort Goudry, canvas bag in his left hand and revolver in his right was midway across the room heading for a door which led on to an alleyway at the rear of the building. On the floor behind him stood a small iron safe, its door open to display empty shelves. When he recognized Charlie his mouth opened in wonderment. 'You!' he said, the word carrying a conviction that Charlie was the architect of his downfall. He swung the gun in Charlie's direction and pulled the trigger.

The bullet was off-target, smacking into the wood of the door some inches above Charlie's head. Charlie drew back into the shelter of the recess, out of sight of his adversary, but another bullet buried itself into the wall to his left.

Cocking his pistol, Charlie re-entered the room by diving low on to the floor.

He fired at the point where Mort Goudry had last stood but he was no longer there. The room was now empty, the outside door stood open and Charlie cursed the fact that the man had slipped away. When he was joined by Fess Salter they could hear the scuffle of men in their wake, men aroused by the swamper's tale of woe and the sound of gunfire from the backroom.

Cautiously, Charlie and Fess went outside. Any expected gun shots failed to materialize. Beyond the door was a narrow alley which provided no suitable place for a man to wait in ambush. Because townspeople were gathered at the main street end of the alley it was clear that Goudry had gone deeper into the maze of narrow passages at the rear of the buildings. They paused and listened and Fess picked up the sound of a horse somewhere to their right. They raced along the alley and through a narrow gap between two buildings they caught a glimpse of Goudry astride a grey.

'Stop,' yelled Fess who fired a shot over Goudry's head to back up the command, but it was ignored. Goudry, struggling to secure the canvas bag to his saddle, turned and fired his own gun in reply. Charlie and Fess knew that they would be walking into a death trap if they tried to reach him via that gap as it was barely wide enough to accommodate them in single file. In a moment he was gone from their sight but they could hear his urgent yells as the horse picked up speed to get clear of town.

'I reckon he'll head for the Revlon farm,' said Fess Salter. 'Fresh horses,' he added in explanation.

They turned back towards the front of the Wild Horse to collect their own horses. One man had detached himself from those congregated at the end of the alley and was advancing at pace, gun in hand, star on shirt.

'What's all the shooting about?' asked Sheriff Bland.

'Mort Goudry,' Charlie answered. 'He's the leader of the Red Mask gang.' Charlie had to give more details and Fess had to produce the document he carried before they were able to convince the doubting lawman that they were acting on behalf of the government. Consequently, Mort Goudry was more than ten minutes ahead when they set off in pursuit.

Already this morning, their mounts had carried them from Arkadelphia and now they were being asked to chase down the fresher animal before it reached Revlon's farm. Fess suspected that Goudry would scatter most of the horses corralled at the farm but with the couple he kept he would probably push on south to New Orleans where a ship could carry him to New York, South America or Europe. Charlie didn't disagree but he knew that the Revlon farm was the extent of his own horse's stamina.

There had been no tracks to follow. The dry ground was scuffed by many animals and it was impossible to identify fresh tracks, especially as speed was essential. They had cut towards higher ground to give themselves a greater panorama of the land ahead but without success. Whatever route Mort Goudry had chosen it was keeping him from their view.

'Have we figured this wrong?' asked Charlie when they reached the crest of a ridge.

'It's possible,' admitted Fess, 'but I can't believe he'd ride north with the army searching the territory for him.'

'Texas?'

'Could be,' said Fess, 'but he'd still be running in this direction to get there.'

Fess shielded his eyes from the high sun to look into the distance. Then, as he was about to urge his horse forward, he paused and pointed to a movement below. Something grey moving awkwardly among the high boulders. Goudry's horse.

Drawing their weapons, they picked a

path down the slope to the spot where they'd seen the horse. The grey was lame and had been abandoned.

Fess scouted around and found some boot prints but not in a line to indicate a direction of flight.

'Could be he's among these boulders hoping to get a bead on us,' said Fess.

'Perhaps he brought an extra horse when he left town,' Charlie said. 'Someone had readied the grey for him.' He was thinking of the stableman who'd been charged with the task of 'telling the boss' when Fess was being taken to Hot Springs. 'Perhaps there was a pack horse, too.'

'Then we need to hurry,' said Fess.

'My horse needs a rest,' Charlie said. Its head hung low and its body was damp with sweat. 'Ten minutes?'

'I'll go on ahead,' said Fess, 'if he scatters the horses at the farm we'll never catch him.'

Although reluctant to allow his friend to ride into danger alone, Charlie was still aware that it would be more reckless to ride his horse into its grave. Ten minutes lost now was better than finding himself afoot with the journey uncompleted. He dismounted and watched as Fess rode away. He poured some water into his hat and let each horse lap at it in turn.

While he screwed the cap on to his canteen a sound came to him from the boulders behind. It was neither a shuffle nor a scratch but it had elements of each. In other circumstances he would have attributed the noise to a small animal but the prospect that Mort Goudry was still in the vicinity caused him to act with caution. He crouched behind his horse, drew his revolver and waited for a recurrence of the sound.

It came again two minutes later, perhaps not an exact replica but similar enough to know that it had been created in the same manner. It was a dragging sound, one unlikely to be made by anything but a human.

Charlie lay on his belly and squirmed

away from the horses, moving to the cover of some boulders to the right of the source of the noise. He paused, listened and began to sweat with the heat of the day. Then a small stone rolled and Charlie knew for certain that there was someone hiding among the rocks. Crouching, he moved again, climbing the rising ground, placing his feet carefully where there were no small stones to disturb or twigs to snap. He found Mort Goudry lying across a boulder which overlooked the place where the horses waited in the shade. He was on his belly with his revolver in his hand. The canvas bag lay close to his left hand, there were scuff marks where it had been pulled from one location to another, the source of the sound that had betrayed his presence.

Mort Goudry raised his head, turned it slightly from side to side trying, Charlie supposed, to locate his enemy.

Charlie, behind him, rose to his feet and pointed his gun at Mort's back. When he spoke he did so slowly, deliberately, making it clear to Mort that he had no other option than to obey his command. 'Drop the gun.'

Mort's shoulders stiffened, his head turned slightly as though about to look back over his shoulder. Charlie cocked his pistol so that the metallic sound left Mort in no doubt that he needed to obey instantly. He did so, tossing the gun to the side and raising his arms. He turned so that he lay on his back then began to sit up.

'If the rifle hadn't been too heavy to carry along with the money I could have shot both of you when you first got here. To be sure with the pistol I needed to be closer. Of course, all I really want is a horse. How about we do a deal? There's a lot of money in this bag,' he pulled it towards him. 'What do you say to a thousand dollars? I heard you telling those brothers that you wanted to return home with money in your pocket so here's your chance.' He opened the bag. 'It's full of money. I'll make it two thousand,' he said. 'Two thousand dollars for you and the horse for me. Nobody will ever know. Tell them I tricked you and stole your horse.'

Charlie was watching him, listening to his words, noting the glint in Mort Goudry's eyes that meant he believed that money was every man's god. Charlie did want money, did want to return to Ruth Prescott with enough to start their own spread on that headland over the Tatanka. That had been their dream but he wouldn't do it with money covered in the blood of the Willis brothers or the terrorised citizens of Pine Bluff and other towns.

'Put up your hands,' he said. 'The army is looking for you.'

Mort Goudry made one more appeal, his hand dipping swiftly into the bag. 'All the money you want,' he said, but the tone of his voice had changed and the hand movement was a grasp for something other than money.

Charlie heard the change in Mort's

voice and understood the desperation that showed in his eyes. Charlie pulled the trigger and as his pistol kicked in his hand the bullet smacked into Mort Goudry's brow. The gun from the money bag fell to the ground and the last of the Red Mask gang was dead.

★　★　★

The death of Mort Goudry deprived the government of the opportunity to publicize their victory with a major trial. Two people were in custody but neither was of a calibre that would reflect glory on the efforts of the army against those who wouldn't allow the war to end. Grant Harbottle, the only survivor of the debacle at Arkadelphia, was a slow-witted lad who rode with the Red Masks because his now-perished older brothers had done so and he knew no other way but to follow them. And the death of her son, Clint, proved to be one personal disaster too many for Mary Rose Revlon. Captain Jessop and his men, who arrived at the farm a handful of minutes ahead of Fess Salter, found a physically exhausted and mentally incapable woman lying in the yard near a partly dug grave. Prison awaited both Grant Harbottle and Mary Rose Revlon so, for a true testimony of their determination to crush other rebel bands, the army would have to depend on word of mouth and deeds like those at Arkadelphia.

However, the role played by Charlie Jefferson and Fess Salter in the destruction of the Red Mask gang was not overlooked. Word came that a bonus payment awaited them at Fort Smith.

'Will it be enough to send you back to the Wyoming Territory?' Fess asked his friend.

It was a start to the fortune he hoped to build, Charlie thought, but not nearly enough to finance the home he planned to share with Ruth Prescott.

'Do you think Colonel Crook can

still use me?' he asked.

'I'm sure of it,' said Fess. 'Another of 'Bloody Bill' Anderson's men is running a gang up in Missouri, a fellow called Archie Clements, the colonel will be happy if we can destroy that one, too.'

★ ★ ★

Charlie Jefferson and Fess Salter rode into Hot Springs three days later, a detour that Charlie insisted they make before they completed their journey to Fort Smith. One or two heads turned in their direction as they rode slowly along the street but Charlie thought it unlikely that these people knew the part he and Fess had played in the destruction of the Red Mask gang. Even so, when he reined in outside the mercantile store and stepped down from the saddle he had an uneasy feeling. Perhaps he was wrong to do what he was about to do but he had deceived Harriet Galbraith and needed to free his conscience of that burden.

Harriet was serving a customer but when she saw him enter her smile showed pleasure and relief. Charlie suspected that she hadn't expected to see him again. He removed his hat, held it by the brim and waited for her to finish serving the customer.

'We haven't seen you for a few days,' she began.

'I've been busy.'

'Have you found work?'

'I have a job.'

'Then you'll be around town for a while.'

'No,' he said. 'I'm here to say goodbye.'

'Oh!'

'But there is something I need to tell you before I go.'

She examined his face. 'Is it really so serious?'

He nodded. 'You'll be hurt by what I tell you. Perhaps your father should hear this too.'

She looked over her shoulder to

where her father was busy filling a customer's order. 'Just tell me,' she said.

So Charlie told her that he was a government agent whose task it had been to destroy the Red Mask gang.

'I didn't kill your brother,' he told her, 'but I was involved in the skirmish in which he died. I brought his body into town to flush out other gang members.'

'Did you have a hand in the massacre at Arkadelphia?' she asked.

'Yes.'

'I've seen the list of people killed. Some of them were from Hot Springs, men from good families.'

'Miss Galbraith,' he said, 'I fought in the war and when Lee surrendered I believed that that was the end of the fighting. But now I know it might continue for years, not because the south can raise another army but because individuals will seize the opportunity to hide behind past grievances for their own gain. I told you once that I am as much opposed to the immoral behaviour of the carpetbaggers as I am the violence of the bushwhackers. That is the truth, and if I had the means to instantly wipe away all the evil in the land I would do so, but I haven't. I can only tackle one obstacle at a time.'

'Does that mean that you're not going back to your Wyoming home?'

'Not yet. Like a lot of people, my friend Amos died in the belief that the cause he fought for was the true cause. The north won so I reckon my debt to him is to give the victory he bought a chance to work.'

Charlie replaced his hat, went outside and climbed back on his horse. Then he and Fess headed north to meet Colonel Crook at Fort Smith.